ON PARLIAMENT HILL

Other Works by Ian Gouge

Novels and Novellas

A Pattern of Sorts - Coverstory books, 2020
The Opposite of Remembering - Coverstory books, 2020
At Maunston Quay - Coverstory books, 2019
An Infinity of Mirrors - Coverstory books, 2018 (2nd ed.)
The Big Frog Theory - Coverstory books, 2018 (2nd ed.)
Losing Moby Dick and Other Stories - Coverstory books, 2017

Short Stories

Degrees of Separation - Coverstory books, 2018
Secrets & Wisdom - Paperback, 2017

Poetry

The Homelessness of a Child - Coverstory books, 2021
The Myths of Native Trees - Coverstory books, 2020
First-time Visions of Earth from Space - Coverstory books, 2019
After the Rehearsals - Coverstory books, 2018
Punctuations from History - Coverstory books, 2018
Human Archaeology - Paperback, 2017
Collected Poems (1979-2016) - KDP, 2017

Anthologies

New Contexts: 1 - Coverstory books, 2020
Triple Measures - Ian Gouge, K.M.Miller, Tom Furniss, Coverstory books, 2020
Oak Tree Alchemy - Coverstory books, 2019
Play for Three Hands - Tom Furniss, Ian Gouge, K.M.Miller, 1981

IAN GOUGE

ON PARLIAMENT HILL

Coverstory books

Published by Coverstory books, 2021

ISBN 978-19162899-8-7 (paperback)

ISBN 978-19162899-9-4 (ebook)

Copyright © Ian Gouge 2021

The cover image of Parliament Hill
was designed by the author © Ian
Gouge 2021.

www.iangouge.com

www.coverstorybooks.com

b

One

Her voice had carried him back. There was no definable accent to speak of, no specific twang or rise and fall, no mannerisms to mark it out as distinctive or exceptional. Neither was it the words she uttered; they were merely window-dressing. What he continues to hear, what provokes memory, are elements beyond the vocal: confidence, honesty, inquisitiveness. Perhaps openness most of all. It is the sound of an adventurer, of someone who, knowing themselves precisely and certain of the ground upon which they stand, are comfortable seeking out new people and new experiences. For some it might have been construed a compulsion, a mission, an addiction.

He had been regarded as a new person once before; being a subject of interest was a novelty bestowed on him unexpectedly - and in Cath's case almost literally 'out-of-the-blue'. And when endowed with such an attribute how could he have done anything other than explore it, to test and tease at it to see where it might lead? It had been Cath's voice which turned him into an explorer too.

But that was then. Fourteen years ago. Yet this is now, and he is so much older - and so unprepared...

No, perhaps not unprepared. Anaesthetised, perhaps, having spent much of the intervening period between then and now putting up barriers, building walls, establishing defences in such a way as to prevent his citadel ever being breached again. Even so - and after all that time and effort - here is a second voice of undefinable and undeniable quality suddenly confronting him.

Inevitably, anaesthetic wears off.

3

Harry has stood alongside him as an occasional confessor, watching this new assailant gathering strength, deciphering and unpicking Neil's life; and in attempting to help, Harry has divulged whys and wherefores, though perhaps too often Neil has chosen not to listen. That is also a replay of the past. "It's because you're nearly thirty-six" he recalls Harry saying not that long ago, "because on one level your life is fundamentally unsatisfying; because there is a gap in it - in your life, in you - which has grown gradually like a cancer. And even if you choose not to recognise all of that, choose not to see it, that doesn't mean those things are not there, things that need to be addressed, sorted out, lanced like a boil." And though his friend may not have spoken those exact words, he had given him clue enough. Yet still Neil had chosen to stand, hands thrust in his pockets, looking out from his castle, pretending he was safe, secure.

Until now.

✺

"Do you often take photographs like that?"

The voice came suddenly from above and behind him, a rich and strangely sonorous music intruding on the moment. He steadied himself, held his breath, then pressed the shutter release. The reassuring 'click' of capture. Lowering the camera from his eye, he rolled to his right and onto his side; looked up.

Silhouetted against the sun, he could make out nothing of her, only the indistinct shape of a figure, its perspective distorted by his viewing angle and the blurred halo of sunlight that enveloped her. He tried to corral the image for sometime later. From her outline he could tell she was looking down at him, waiting for a response. He was thrown, unnerved a little; all he had was her sound and for an instant he tried to place it, analyse it, then gave up.

"Sometimes," he offered, then rolled back onto his front and stared out over London wondering - without the camera to his eye this time - if he had managed to frame the trees in the foreground as he had hoped, left them sufficiently out-of-focus to create the depth he was looking for. And also wondering who the girl was that belonged to the voice, and why she was suddenly there talking to him.

"Does it work?"

Now the voice was closer, the distance between them halved; he sensed she had crouched down a little, trying to imagine what he had seen or had been trying to photograph.

"Often enough."

She laughed.

"You sound confident," she said, her tone light and playful, "like you know what you're doing."

He shifted onto his side again. She was looking not at him but at the skyline, North London spread beneath their Parliament Hill vantage point, here and there the sun glinting off random windows, the towers of the city seemingly within touching distance. He registered a white t-shirt, denim shorts.

"Can I see?"

She looked back at him - or rather at his camera - her question suggesting there was a truth he had locked within it, one to which she wanted access. He wondered if she was asking if she could take the camera from him, try it out, peer through the viewfinder to see if she could divine what he had seen; but if that had been the case she would have been holding out her hand too, backing up her request with a gesture. And then he realised her eyes were more focussed and had settled on the three-by-two display on the camera's back where an image would appear for two seconds after the shot, simultaneously stored in all its pixelated glory on the sim card to await later analysis.

They were the eyes that belonged to the voice. Probably brown - but vaguely grey in the strong shadow that shrouded her face - they too seemed confident and assured, though of what he was unable to decide. They moved from the camera to his own. He held them for a split second, then glanced at the Canon himself.

"There's no point. You can't see anything worthwhile on this. And especially not in this light. The photo needs to be seen on a bigger screen, where the definition's good."

"Then why is it there, if there's no point in it?"

It was his turn to laugh. He sat up and faced her, cradling the camera in his lap.

"Because it does more than just show you the picture you've just taken. Some people actually use it as a viewfinder - though I've never been able to. For me there's no substitute for getting your eye up close; that's how you feel you are a photographer. But the screen's also where you can see all the settings for the shot; the speed and aperture for example, or the burst rate if you're taking something that's moving like a car or a runner. It's a bit like a menu on a computer I suppose. In a way these things are computers."

"Show me," she said as she turned her crouch into something else, kneeling alongside him, her legs tucked under her.

As he lifted the camera and tilted its back toward her, he tried to take her in, to open his internal shutter to add more elements to the composite image he was trying to build. Her hair was light brown, cut slightly shorter than was the modern norm; it was shaped to suit her slightly elongated face and complimented her eyes and the shape of her cheeks. Her lips were a little thin but not unappealing, and as she waited he saw concentration generate the smallest furrow of a frown on her forehead.

"Look" he said, pressing the menu button and bringing the screen to life.

✿

"Between Kentish Town and Chalk Farm," he answered. "I often come up here onto the Heath to take pictures. The number twenty-four stops not far from my road so getting here takes no time at all."

As they walked down Parliament Hill itself, past solid three- and four-storey middle-class London semis, heading for a café she knew near the Royal Free, she had asked him where he lived. It was a question that perfectly fitted the sequence their meeting had initiated.

Having shown her a little of the subtleties and intricacies of his camera, they had chatted for a while about inconsequential things. He found himself fascinated by the tone of her voice, its rhythm, the way she spoke. It had lured him in, ensnared him almost, well before he had appreciated just how pretty she was. Or perhaps her voice had somehow enhanced her beauty. Yet although they talked, she disclosed little, their conversation driven by her delving.

"Do you take photographs of people?" she had asked while they were still on the hill, just as he began to worry their exchange was drying up.

"Yes," he said, laughing again, "of course."

"Then you may take my picture," she said as if she were granting him permission, and graciously reclined on the grass, "and as a fee I will let you buy me a coffee - if that is an acceptable arrangement."

He had taken four when she suddenly laughed and started to adopt exaggerated poses, changing them rapidly, forcing him to shoot quickly. In less than a minute she had been on her feet.

"I think that's enough, don't you? Can you afford more than one coffee?"

It was a laugh that married her voice.

"I know some people might think it's a bit of a hike, but do you sometimes walk up here when the weather's fine? I mean it sounds as if your place is not that far from Gospel Oak and you can get into the park from there." This as they neared the bottom of the hill, following on from the disclosure of his domicile.

"Yes, sometimes I do, why?"

That she lived in Gospel Oak was the first question she answered. That her name was Cath was the second.

"It's Catherine, of course" - they were sitting in a small café within sight of the terminal stop of the twenty-four bus - "but I've always felt that was a little too cumbersome. Too many syllables. My family still use it, much to my annoyance, and I can't escape that at the moment; but I've always seen myself as a Cath. I tried Katy, even Cat for a while, but Cath is what I've settled on." She paused. "What do you think?"

"Me?"

"Am I a Catherine or a Cath? Or a Cat, a Katy, a Cathy?"

He laughed.

"I don't know."

"But you must have a view. Don't they say that we weigh other people up in something ridiculous like the first eleven seconds of meeting? And you've had at least half an hour! I'd say your opinion is valid - and I won't charge you for giving it to me!"

He had only one answer available to him.

※

As they waited at the bus stop, Cath's attention was momentarily caught by the arrival of an ambulance at the hospital, it's siren cutting through the mid-afternoon thrum. In taking the opportunity to re-evaluate her, to frame her almost, Neil tried as best he could to be detached and objective. It was a skill he was trying to hone when it came to taking photographs, to focus on what he was seeing and not how he felt about what he was seeing. In Cath's case such an endeavour could only be partially successful. Their time face-to-face in the café had served to enhance his initial impression that she was an attractive young woman, and the style in which she had her hair cut - and the way she would regularly tuck stray strands of it behind her left ear exposing a colourful enamelled earring in the shape of a bird - could do nothing but endorse that view. Consistent with her slightly elongated face, she was taller than average, the primary reason for this being the length of her legs which had remained hidden sitting on the hill and only truly revealed themselves as they walked away from it, Neil dropping behind her on occasion to allow pedestrians going up the hill to pass.

"Penny for your thoughts." Her voice roused him.

"Sorry, I was miles away."

She nodded towards Fleet Road.

"Here comes your bus."

Although they had established that the twenty-four would have been perfectly suitable to take her at least part of the way home, she had previously settled on a stroll up Hampstead High Street and intended to stick to her plan. There had been a moment when Neil had wondered whether he should offer to accompany her - even tried to weigh-up whether she wanted him to do so - but that passed in a fraction of uncertainty, an aperture over which he had no control whatsoever. However, her waiting with him for the bus felt like a second prize worth having.

"When can I see the photos?" she asked, drawing him back from the large red Routemaster heading their way.

"The photos?"

"From the hill. I want to see how good a job you did up there."

In terms of any next step, he had processed nothing beyond his failure to extend their acquaintance to include the High Street.

"I rarely print any out," he said, slightly at sea, "so it's not as if I'll have a pack of six-by-fours to show you."

"And I'm guessing they would be inadequate anyway?"

He nodded.

"Then I'll have to see them on a screen of some kind, won't I?"

He was suddenly conscious of the bus - its indicator flashing - being very close; it felt threatening, as if its arrival would bring their encounter to a premature end, popping it like a pin in a balloon and leaving him with only shattered remnants.

"I could put some on a memory stick and bring them to your place."

She laughed as if that was the most ridiculous suggestion she'd ever heard.

"I don't think so," she said, in an incredulous rather than a malicious way. She looked away from him to dip into the small bag she carried over her shoulder, and pulled out a pen and a small notebook.

As the bus came to a halt in front of them, he watched her fingers flit across the paper creating a sequence of numbers out of nothing.

"Here," she said, tearing the sheet from the book and handing it to him. "When you're happy with the photos call me and we'll arrange for me to come and see them. If that's ok."

He took the paper, the numbers instantly blurring before his eyes and making him wonder whether they would ever sort themselves out.

"Yes. Perfect."

❖

And now he has come back. After all this time. Pulled back by a voice; another voice; a similar voice.

Having made both decision and invitation, he had debated the best route to take across the heath to get him to their designated meeting point. Immobile and imperious, it rises over its segment of North London as it always has, and although there have been some changes in the general environs (the café near the Royal Free is now a vape shop, for example) much of its supporting framework remains the same. Nothing drastic has happened to the buildings on Parliament Hill; the overground from Gospel Oak to Hampstead Heath still runs at its foot, and even if the old Routemasters have recently started to disappear, their routes remain, the number twenty-four a constant beyond diesel technology.

In the end he eschewed the entrance from Parliament Hill itself, and walked up via the bathing ponds. It is a route he has taken frequently enough not to be on his guard for anything new. Given he has returned to the hill first to think and then to speak, it seemed appropriate he leave his mind unclouded for as long as possible.

That had been the plan.

Standing near the viewpoint and looking out over a London that has metamorphosed so much more than the hill itself, Neil hears Cath's first words as clearly as if she were standing just behind him once again. Not only does he hear her question, he cannot help but overlay Beth's voice onto it as if they have become an amalgam, two people fused together through a shared attribute. Or a common denominator.

Knowing he was coming back, he still managed to avoid digging out from one of his many electronic archives the photographs of the city he had taken back then - from just over there, wasn't it? - laying on his stomach, engaged in what has subsequently proved to be a perennial struggle for composition. It had occurred to him to compare and contrast, as if doing so might have grounded him with a cross-reference other than one compromised of voices and his memory; something substantive and reliable, certain and unquestionable. Neil thinks he recalls it well enough however, and a for a few seconds tries to reframe the image. He is not exactly sure how much the trees have grown since then, but given they must have done so, presumably the photograph would look subtly different were he to take it today. From within his pocket his mobile phone nags at him momentarily, reminding him that he has the means to recapture it should he wish to do so. It is an offer he declines, pulling it out merely to switch it to silent. In any event, he knows the hill has lost a few trees to storms and disease in the last thirteen years, so how much of a replica could he create anyway? And it is not replication he is after. Quite the opposite.

Although the vacant bench on which he chooses to wait is set facing slightly more east than south, he is able to sit in such a way to allow the heart of the city to occupy the centre of his view. Having done so, he imagines - rather than deliberately picks out - Gospel Oak, Kentish Town and Camden between him and the silver towers down by the river; locates - generally if not specifically - Haverstock Hill and Eversholt Street and the dark green smudge of Regent's Park. Confusingly appearing to be on a level with him, he watches planes on their final descent into Heathrow. There is comfort in the predictability of it all - and disquiet in that every element of the scene is a trigger for both memories and questions.

He had thought he was done with questions. Not day-to-day mundane decision-making - what to wear, where to eat, where to go on holiday - but the 'big' questions, the ones that carried significance and whose answers really mattered. Unlike those posed in his professional life - relating to subject, lighting, depth of field - he has managed to avoid 'important' ones by constructing an existence which means they don't get asked in the first place, relegated to a sphere where - based on an internal and invisible method of calculation - they are turned from questions into something else. It took him half a year to construct such a philosophy, one that has served him well for the majority of the last six or so.

But now, it seems this philosophy may no longer be valid; now he must put himself back in the frame.

❀

"You've made me look beautiful."

"I didn't really do anything."

He meant it as a compliment, spoken almost before he had given himself the chance to weigh-up the words and decide if they were the right ones to utter. Although truthful at one level, on another Neil was being dishonest. He had made multiple copies of the photos he had taken of her, duplicated them on his computer so that he could edit each image in subtly different ways, applying ranges of masks, hues and tints, trying out effects to soften or sharpen, and cropping to create various locations for the centre of focus. As ever, it was as if he expected there to be a combination which, were he able to find it, would unlock treasure. Other than superficially, his efforts made little difference however. Most of the photographs were good enough - and Cath looked wonderful in all of them. Where she had posed and moved, where he had been forced to snap quickly, those were undoubtedly the best, filled with life and humour. Filled with her wonderful legs.

Before settling on the selection he would show her, he had tried them out on Harry. All of them.

"Shit, she's gorgeous!" It had been a typically enthusiastic Harry-type response. He clicked through them all, pausing longer on some than others. Neil made a mental note where he had dallied.

"And she just came up and started talking to you?"

"Yes."

"She must have liked the look of your arse!"

Neil had explained the circumstance of their meeting.

"Of course you realise to an uneducated eye this lot looks more like stalking than photography, more obsession than anything else..."

"I'm just trying to get it right." But even as he spoke, Neil knew the truth was somewhere between extremes.

Having eventually chosen just twelve - eight photographs of Cath to accompany two he had taken of the skyline (including the very one she had interrupted) plus two from earlier in the day - he had decided to take her through them in chronological sequence, largely to get her reaction on something that didn't matter, and then - with hers last - on something that really did.

❀

"What happened next?"

Keen to understand how it had worked out, Harry rang him the following day.

"Nothing too dramatic."

"'Nothing too dramatic'?" he echoed, unable to keep incredulity from his voice. "You've just played probably the best chat-up gambit in the history of chat-up gambits - you've made the girl think she's beautiful, for Christ's sake! - and you tell me nothing happened! I don't believe it."

"I didn't say nothing *at all* happened…"

Neil is sure he doesn't recall their exchange perfectly, but from a distance of many years it's close enough.

Hearing a shout, he turns his head to the right to see a father running after his son who is cycling inexpertly across the grass. A first bike. The Heath is a popular spot for such learner-driving, though Neil wonders if in this case the two aren't a little too close to where the hill starts to sweep downwards. Catching up to the boy, the father and arrests his progress by grabbing the back of the bicycle seat. There is laughter. He turns the boy around and then, jogging, starts him off again up toward the crest. They will have disappeared in a minute.

Something *had* happened; of course it had. They had looked at the photographs for a little while, Cath occasionally asking questions as to how certain effects had been achieved. Neil had shown her some of the features of his Photoshop software, allowed her to experiment on a couple of shots of horses he had taken on holiday the previous year. He made some remark about how clever it all was but that you needed something special to work with in the first place. The particular phrase he used has blurred beyond recognition - either that or he was so embarrassed by it that he has condemned it to oblivion. He had been trying to find a way to replay his first sentiment, confirming that she was beautiful, that the photos couldn't lie and neither could he. He had been trying to tell her something for which both words and pictures were inadequate.

They had gone for a walk. Her suggestion. It had been a rambling, incoherent kind of walk which eventually led them to Camden Market, bustling on a Saturday afternoon. A week had passed since the hill. They'd had a coffee and then browsed the shops and stalls, and at one point - he still can't remember exactly when, where or how - she was holding his hand. He didn't let it go until he saw her onto the north-bound train at Camden Road station. She had kissed him, briefly, softly, and said "Thank you".

Replaying it now, even with the natural abrasion of time between he and the events themselves, Neil can't help but feel the episode otherworldly, as if he were enacting something taken from 'Mills and Boon', a romantic encounter so off-the-scale it couldn't possibly be true. But he had pinched himself often enough in those early and heady days to know it was indeed real; and now he had the collateral of what followed - the good and the bad - to evidence he hadn't just made it up. And he'd had Harry's approval: "you lucky bastard!". Once again staring out across London's rooftops, remembering and waiting, past and future fused to the same spot, he recognised not without gratitude the value of Harry's testimony; it was a compass to help him navigate.

At that embryonic moment with Cath, he and Harry had known each other long enough - four years since they met during their final year at the LSE - for Neil to have weighed him up, to have the measure of him. And vice versa. To some, Harry could be over-exuberant, too keen, a bit 'mouthy' and self-opinionated. He could be a little quick to things: to judge, to anger, to dismiss. But he had proven himself a decent yardstick, a mirror against which Neil could hold things up and get a true reflection. For all Harry's faults, integrity - overlooked by many - was his defining characteristic. And so when Harry passed judgement on Cath - or on him as far as Cath's potential was concerned - Neil listened. He might have made a show of dismissing the proclamations and bluster, but he seldom truly ignored what Harry said.

Well, not until it was too late.

As far as he can now recall, the next few weeks, the crescendo of that high summer, passed in something of a haze. The next time Cath came to visit him - the following day in fact - they made love for the first time; a strangely hesitant and blundering experience is how he imagines it now. After that, they spent most of every weekend together, mainly walking and exploring. Cath loved to explore; even with places she knew well she would strive for a new perspective, a different angle. They would go to museums and galleries over and over, at her insistence taking different routes through them each time to see if the sequence in which you came upon the exhibits changed your appreciation of them. She had a notion that the response to any painting in the National Gallery could alter depending on whether you approached it from left or right, or what you had seen immediately before. It was almost as if she were trying to surprise them - and as such it was part of her charm.

It has been years since he has been in the National Gallery. As he sits, Neil tries to pick out its approximate location. He knows if he is able to locate Big Ben, then it will be somewhere near there, camouflaged by the thoroughfares of Oxford Street and Tottenham Court Road. He puts a hand up to shield the sun from his eyes as if that will make a difference and isolate his target piece from the jigsaw puzzle that is the City.

Once more - inevitably, perhaps - he is attracted by the thread of aircraft as they descend from the east, homing-in on Heathrow. If he looked further to the right he knows he could watch them as they rose into the air, heading off around the world; yet it is arrival which fascinates him more. Is that natural, he wonders; do most people do the same? Or does it say something about him and the lure of 'coming home'? If so, it is a bias that has not always been there; perhaps it is a new preoccupation, driven by circumstance or a fresh desire.

Questions. As if they have suddenly appeared to prove a point, once again there are questions.

✿

"We should go away. On holiday."

He had made the statement one Sunday evening as they sat on his sofa flicking through tv channels trying to find something to occupy the last half-an-hour before Cath made her way home.

She preferred her Sunday returns to be solitary journeys. On a few occasions Neil had accompanied her to the end of her Gospel Oak road, but he had yet to be invited any further. Her front door remained a navy blue blur part-way along the smart terrace of mews-type houses. Cath had begged for patience. Her claim that she was still warming-up her parents "to the idea of him" only succeeded in raising the spectre that whilst *he* was already 'all in' as far as their relationship was concerned, Cath might yet have reservations. Having defined the boundaries of it, he wondered if she had become too comfortable with the routine she had prescribed for them. He wanted to ask her about moving in with him, but given he had yet to make it across the threshold of her current home, that felt a step too far.

The notion of a holiday and their removal from the domestic to the international, launching themselves into the wider world as a twosome without the comfort-blanket and familiarity of North London and their regular haunts, felt to Neil as if it might prove something - to Cath as much as him.

She sat up.

"I was thinking the same thing!"

"You were?"

"You sound surprised." She laughed. "But I didn't suggest it because I wasn't sure."

"About what?"

"Oh, I don't know." Glancing away from him and looking in a vague way around the room, her eyes settled on the clock ticking away on the mantlepiece. She placed her hand on his knee and squeezed it gently. "Whether it was too soon, I suppose?"

"For who?"

It was a big question encapsulated in two small words.

"Where did you have in mind?" she continued, swerving his question.

"Nowhere really," he said, then tried to sound more constructive. "I mean anywhere but the UK. I've still got some holiday I could take, and the second half of September might be good because the kids are back at school and so things will be less expensive."

"And less busy, too."

He said nothing, waiting for her response.

"Anywhere?" she asked.

"Within reason," he smiled. "We need to be able to get there and back in a week, and we need to be able to afford it. So long-haul's probably out of the question, as is Monaco."

"My favourite place!" she said, playfully, then allowed a short pause. "Italy. I've always wanted to go to Italy. Florence. Tuscany. Somewhere like that. How would that be?"

His own hankering was for northern France, particularly Picardy. Or possibly southern Belgium. For some time now, convinced he could make a decent fist of it, he had wanted to undertake a photographic project with war cemeteries at its heart. He imagined a portfolio - or even an exhibition! - where his images would offer a modern and unique slant on the subject, one which would enhance the graves' poignancy and make the message they encapsulated even more powerful. It was a grand ambition. In anticipation - and for some reason assuming Cath would have no specific preference to outweigh his own - he had even undertaken research, going as far as to investigate options for travel, places to stay, an itinerary for a week. That she had so quickly and strongly settled on northern Italy took him a little by surprise.

"We were supposed to go when I was a little younger - probably eight or ten years ago now - but for some reason I can't recall we never made it. I think it was to do with Daddy's job. He had often been there when he was younger and used to talk about the cathedrals and galleries, the countryside, the rivers flowing through Pisa and Florence, the vineyards - and the ice cream!"

Joining the dots, Neil linked this small slice of biography with Cath's obvious preferences when they were walking the National Gallery.

"Have you ever been?"

He shook his head.

"I know you can fly to Pisa or Florence - or even fly into one and back from the other. I'm sure the weather will be great in September. And I think if my father finds out you are taking me to Italy, well…"

✿

As he recalls it now, watching another plane on its silent and gradual glide into Heathrow, he remembers how she had let that final phrase hang unfinished in the air, the power and potential of it. Then, as now, it felt akin to facing the final trump card you had miscounted, or the sudden and unexpected slide of a bishop or a rook to unmask a devastating check. If he had wondered at the time whether Cath's move was a calculated one, he has lost that reference, and yet another replaying of the scene leaves him with only his standard conclusion: he remains satisfied she was simply being genuine, enthusiastic, honest.

Voices nearby grab his attention. A couple have come to a standstill a few yards from him, pausing to look across the city. Arm-in-arm, the young man is using his free hand to point things out, and though Neil cannot hear exactly what is being said he can imagine the list of highlights he is working through. The presentation is punctuated by comments from his companion, her words delivered in a heavy southern European accent. Influenced by his own preoccupations at that precise moment, for a split second Neil wonders if she might be Italian, but then manages to filter out a few words. Spanish.

He and Cath had talked about Spain too that evening, working through the list of possibilities both as they sat on the sofa and then subsequently during the short walk to Kentish Town West station. Having nailed her Italian colours firmly to the mast, Neil had worked through his own destination preferences. She had dismissed northern France and the Low Countries fairly readily, her objection being a lack of 'suitable' culture; at that point he chose not to mention his war graves project. Spain - and particularly Barcelona for the Gaudí - fared a little better, although without any firm substantiation Cath suggested it was the kind of place more mature people went. As he watches the sightseeing couple walk away, he realises he didn't know then - as he still does not today - whether Cath meant 'more mature' in the sense of being physically older, or in that their relationship was more firmly established. Ultimately it only succeeded in making it to a bucket-list of places they were never to visit.

He tried Switzerland for the mountains - too expensive - and Portugal for the beaches - too common - and when he finally resorted to Greece for the ruins, he realised the only thing he could do was capitulate. Did it matter? Having accepted Tuscany before Cath had boarded the train to take her the one stop home, he had rationalised his concession by telling himself it didn't. Surely the most important thing was that they were going somewhere together. On holiday. As long as it was outside of

London, what did it matter where they spent the time? Scenery was just scenery, and wherever they were he would take photographs and they would walk hand-in-hand, laugh, smile, eat and sleep together. The destination was surely just nuance, gloss; if he accepted that, then why shouldn't he have conceded graciously and let Cath get her way?

With the benefit of hindsight and the experience they subsequently shared, he has no idea why he should have been so reticent. Naivety, probably. Now that he knows it better, he has come to love Italy, and has returned a number of times over the past few years, sometimes with work, sometimes on vacation. Recalling Latinate images, he sees mental contact sheets comprising the photographs he has taken playing like a slideshow through his memory.

But sitting on the hill once more and over a decade later, he also sees how there was so much more about that evening than simply the choice of a holiday destination. When he compares the Neil he is now to the one who walked back to his flat that night, he is struck by how little his former self knew. Or rather how much he has been forced to learn in the interim. And he knows learning is painful. The young couple he has just seen, the cycling boy and his father, two girls on a bench nearby just reading, people walking their dogs - everyone is still learning, and still experiencing pain.

He looks at his watch to check how long it is to his next lesson. A memory of Harry appears unbidden, a conversation recent enough as to be relevant to this very day.

"So what are you going to do this time?" Harry had asked abruptly.

"What do you mean, 'this time'?"

The journey of Harry's pint from the table to his lips was arrested by Neil's counter-question and he replaced his glass on a beer-mat.

"Déjà vu, surely?"

"In what sense?"

"Come on!" Harry plainly couldn't work out whether Neil's apparent failure to grasp the situation was genuine or not. He might have been toying with him, but Harry knew that wasn't Neil's usual modus operandi. "This is a big call. Another big call. I just want you to be sure - whatever you decide."

"Is there something to decide?"

"Isn't there? If you think there isn't, then you're probably the only one. Things have moved on. Whether you intended to be or not, you're back on the merry-go-round, Old Fruit; the question is whether you're going to get off or stay on. And on or off, how you go about it."

Neil reflected on how rarely Harry actually used his name. 'Old Fruit' was one of the regular substitutes. He wasn't sure where it had come from nor when Harry had first used it, but he attributed it to some element of his childhood, perhaps an appellation heard when he was growing-up. Although dated, Neil felt the quaintness of it suited Harry as speaker more than he as its target.

"I'm not saying that there isn't a question to answer, Harry. Of course there's a question to answer, merry-go-round or not. But this isn't the same. There's no point talking about Cath or drawing parallels with her because that was an age ago. I was a different person then."

Although he had tried to be assertive, definitive, Neil had expected a rebuttal because he knew Harry didn't agree, that from their individual perspectives the view was subtly different.

He allows his gaze to wander as he recalls the exchange. People, trees, grass, the city. The same component parts now as last week, last month; as all those years ago. And how they appear, in themselves and in relation to each other, depends on where you are standing - or sitting or lying - and how you look at them. Everything is shaped by how you see it, how you want to see it, and by the relationship you impose on those elements and the experience you bring to that viewing. He has spent years living with that notion, day-in day-out, through the viewfinder of his camera.

If you were to ask people knowledgable enough about such things, they would be able to pick out his most recent photos in an identity parade because the images are invested with his knowledge, his perspective, his style of composition - in some respects they *are* him. He has taken his predilections and beliefs - his philosophy, if you like - and using his camera, layered it over the top of what and who he has seen. His photographs represent not only the world as it is but as he views it; not only the people in it, but his appreciation of them and their place in his incarnation of that world. In the end he believes he has been lucky; lucky in that he has found both a perspective and a means of exploring that perspective which is appreciated by others. It gives him more than an income; it gives him a defence.

But Neil also knows, looking back at the city again - always back to that same view! - that as usual, Harry is as right as he is wrong. How could he have protested that there was no point in drawing parallels when that is precisely what he is doing now, sitting on this well-worn Parliament Hill bench, weighing past and future as if they were commodities on either end of a set of scales.

✹

As soon as they walked through the archway for the first time, the Piazza del Campo suddenly there before them, the only possible reaction was to stop dead to take it all in. It was quiet now, early enough in the morning for crowds not to have yet formed in any great number, late enough in the season to promise some respite from both crush and heat. Although the Palio had been run a month earlier, a frisson from that spectacle yet remained: ghostly presences in the wooden benches which in places still framed the part-time oval racetrack, the rippling of the colourful pennants hanging from the town hall, the *contrades'* shields replicated in windows across the city.

His camera already out, Neil raised it to his eye and started shooting. They would be nothing but tourist images, and he knew when they were back in London he would interrogate them with disappointment, frustrated that he had been able to manage nothing better. Trying unusual angles, cropping key elements, capturing people going about their daily business, framing incongruous objects; all were techniques he had been variously adopting in order to elevate his photographs. But he had to work quickly. In the previous couple of days Cath had demonstrated her patience had a limit, and ensuring there were regular shots of her in front of things - like the Duomo in Florence or Pisa's leaning tower - only gifted him so much credit. As she walked on ahead of him, he knew he would have to be up and out on his own early the next morning - their last in Italy - in order to give himself one final chance for he and his camera to do the place justice. It had been the same everywhere they had stayed.

Not that the holiday had been a disaster. Far from it. As he shouldered his Canon and followed Cath down into the piazza itself, he found himself marvelling that he was there at all - and astonished that he was there with her. Words having never been his strong suit, he struggled to pin down what he felt. They were slippery things, words, with meanings that had a nasty habit of wandering when you least expected it. Once you were beyond the black-and-white confines of 'yes' and 'no' it seemed to him that you were in trouble, needing to step gingerly in the minefield. Pictures were unlike words; pictures showed you the world, snapshots in time of the concrete, of the physical and real. Their subjects may have been out of reach for a whole host of reasons, but they were still *there* and undeniable. What he felt for Cath was, he assumed, undeniably real too; after all, it was something he felt day in, day out. And at times like these, as he walked toward where she had paused, shielding her eyes to look up at the town hall across the square, the subtleties of her figure framed in that simple loose white dress he adored seeing her in, the feeling was especially strong. It had been that way for much of the week. Yet because he absorbed himself in the real and the physical - and because it was impossible to capture what he felt for her no matter the speed or aperture setting - he found himself resorting to words. It was like cavorting with the enemy.

His limited vocabulary offered him only one option: 'love'. Did he love Cath? Was what he felt 'love'? How could he possibly know? It was not the kind of question one could refer to arbitration; there was no independent third party (aka Harry!) who could weigh-up the evidence and measure it against a metric of some sort in order to draw a conclusion. There was no Beaufort scale, no Mohs scale to offer something definitive; there was no 'six' or 'seven' against which to navigate. Perhaps that was why he found himself reverting to the binary. As he got to within a couple of metres of her, Cath turning toward him as he did so, he asked himself once again the question which had been occupying him so much over the past week: did he love her? And as she smiled, held out a hand in expectation of it being met by one of his own, as she looked so radiant in that dress, as he remembered making love to her the previous evening and the first time he had ever seen her naked, there was only one possible answer.

"I think," she said, pulling him close, "that when we get home, it's about time you met my family."

It was as if she had reached her own conclusion, too.

✵

"Did you mean what you said?"

They were walking back to his flat after their third Sunday lunch with her parents, the first since she had moved out to live with him. The talk had primarily been about the possibility of a larger flat somewhere in the Gospel Oak / Kentish Town / Chalk Farm triangle.

Restricted by the space available, Cath had been selective in terms of what she moved with her into Neil's current abode. It felt, she said, more like going on a long holiday than moving home, constrained as she was by how much extra his 'bachelor pad' could accommodate. The need for somewhere larger became evident almost instantly: what had once been perfectly adequate for Neil became cramped over-night, and where there had been room - spaces on a bookcase, even spaces on the floor - there were now none. Indeed, many of the flat surfaces seemed to be doing double-duty. Trading-up would be a challenge as they were limited by their relatively modest incomes, neither of them being in especially well-paid jobs. Cath's work behind the scenes at the British Museum was rewarding only in the intellectual and emotional sense, and Neil - increasingly harbouring ambitions to become a professional photographer, whatever that might take - had deliberately avoided a job which demanded he invest too much of himself in it. The consequence of his strategy was finding himself in an essentially administrative role in Marks & Spencer, imposing limits not only on his prospects but on his pay too. Unlike Cath, his reward came outside of work, and on occasion she expressed incredulity as to how he could devote himself to a job to which he was not committed. She was correct in that he wasn't committed, but wrong to imagine that he was 'devoted' to it in any way.

Rupert Wilson, Cath's unassuming father, proved to be their saviour. The extent of his success in business could in no way be divined from the man himself, nor from the external fabric of the Wilsons' relatively modest terraced house. On his first visit Neil had immediately been struck by the *quality* of it: the decor was subtle, precise and pristine; the furniture solid and exceptionally well-made; and here and there, on walls and shelves, images and objects that quite simply screamed taste. Many were originals, and Neil even recognised one or two names: a Frink, a Sutherland. Although you might never have guessed as much, Wilson was loaded.

Which was particularly good news for his only daughter - and hence, by intimate association, Neil too. Although he kept the proposal sketchy, he offered to cover any increase in rent the couple might face when they moved. Not only that, he had some 'contacts in the business' who might be able to help them locate a suitable dwelling. It was this promise that was ringing in their ears as they left Gospel Oak, her father's declaration turning Cath into an excited chatterbox for at least twenty minutes.

"Said about what?" she asked. "Where we might live? Wanting much more space?"

"No," Neil squeezed her hand. "About me being a really good photographer."

"Did I say that?!" she replied in mock surprise. Confident it was the kind of thing she would have said, she realised the conversation about the flat had driven all other subjects entirely from her mind. "Why wouldn't I have meant it? Why do you ask?"

"Just insecure, I guess. Sometimes I struggle to see it."

"What about that photograph of the dog? That one's brilliant."

He knew the one she meant, of course. They had been leaving the Piazza del Campo and the sun, being particularly bright, had thrown solid black shadows across the scene. Cath had been walking a little way ahead of him and was caught in a luminous corridor. The sudden radiance of her dress contrasting vividly against the sharp-edged black of the shade was too good an opportunity to miss. Slightly closer to him and a little way to the right, two children sat eating ice-creams, their heads turned to watch her walk. He had needed take the shot quickly before Cath was lost to the darkness or the children looked away, and fired off four in quick succession. Only later, when they were back home and he was examining his holiday catalogue, did he notice the dog. In the left foreground, facing away from both Cath and the children, looking out of shot, a mongrel had lifted its leg against a metal post and was pissing. The post and the dog were also in a narrow shaft of sunlight, and, when seen in conjunction with the more romanticised elements of the rest of the photo, provided a striking counterpoint; a commentary almost. The dog's detachment, its disregard for beauty and human conventions was stunningly illustrated.

"It was a lucky shot."

"Perhaps - but it's still brilliant," Cath insisted. "Who else has taken a photograph like it, just there, framed like that? It's not just the dog is it? The composure of it is wonderful, striking; and the dog elevates it to another level. Of course there was an element of luck to it; there was no way you could have stood there and waited for something like that. But it happened, that moment, and you have it."

Neil found it interesting that Cath's interpretation of his work rarely considered the physical and tangible; what appealed to her was the message or emotion behind the image. She wanted to know what the picture was 'saying', and it was that to which she reacted. At least in their consideration of the photo of the dog they were on the same page, speaking the same language.

"You know," she continued after a short pause, "you should send it to Daddy."

"What?"

"The dog photo. Send it to him along with maybe half-a-dozen from the trip, the ones you think are your best."

"Why should I do that?"

She looked at him earnestly.

"Because he's heard me saying how good you are, but I want him to see it for himself. And because he knows people. You heard what he said about the flat. Don't under-estimate him, Neil; never under-estimate him."

Considering she rarely used his name, Neil knew how serious she was about her suggestion - and that he could not deny her.

✳

When he saw it for the first time he was stunned. They had agreed to take out virtually all the colour so that, in its black-and-whiteness, the contrast would be even greater; and they had settled on printing it at a standard 6:4 ratio, with the long side a massive one metre wide.

It dominated his little group of five hung on a small section of the gallery wall, flanked by two smaller photos on either side. It more than dominated; it shouted into the room. Cath's figure glowed in the centre of the image, her dress almost a light source. And then the viewer notices the children staring, watching her move, as if they have been so entranced they have forgotten about their ice-creams. And finally, as you allow your eye to be led around the picture by the lines scored across it in the battle between light and dark, you settle on the dog; the impassive, detached, pissing dog. It almost takes your breath away.

"Happy?" Charles, the curator of the exhibition, asked the day before they opened. He had allowed Neil a few moments to take in what they had done to his small contribution to 'Europe: Modern Contexts'. "I don't need to tell you we think this one of the strongest pieces in the show."

But he was wrong. Neil *did* need to be told that. It was all very well him thinking it, or Cath telling him that he was good, but validation by an independent third party was priceless. The image and the subsequent reaction of people who saw it made him whole. During parts of the first day Neil returned again and again to the room where the pissing dog hung, standing against an opposite wall, watching those seeing it for the first time. Most paused longer in front of his picture than any other there, and the majority of those at some point raised a hand, extended a finger, pointed at the dog. Mentally he captured their smiles and laughs, just as he had captured the animal; from off-stage, unseen. It was life imitating art.

Cath had been right about her father, of course. He agreed with her about Neil's photographs - and he did know 'people'. He knew Charles Watson, or someone else who knew Charles, and thus about his forthcoming show. "I've seen your photos and I'd like to use them" had been Charles' opening line. Akin to an impressionable young woman being chatted-up by Casanova or Valentino, Neil had been powerless.

※

When it came, as unexpected as the first, the second call kicked open the door into which Charles' show had allowed Neil to get a foot. He hadn't heard of James Montague either - "Monty to my friends!" - but within a few minutes' conversation found he had landed a small commission.

"I saw your photo at the 'Modern Contexts' thing," Monty said, not mentioning the specific picture as if it were self-evident the one to which he was referring. "Very sharp. Perceptive. They all were, of course. And then later I spoke to Charles Watson. Did a little digging. And here we are."

He spoke in a strange staccato with short punchy sentences, his brevity and editing out of superfluous words resulting a machine-gun-like delivery. As he recalls it, Neil remembers how, in order to truly understand what Monty was saying, he had to both listen and fill in the gaps simultaneously. He mastered it soon enough - and a few months' practice eventually made it second nature.

From his present perch - about which he is beginning to feel somewhat proprietorial - Neil scans the hill as if Monty will suddenly appear, magicked into his presence. But just as he wasn't expecting his call then, it isn't Monty he is waiting for now.

"One of the features' editors at *Condé Nast*," Monty had said when introducing himself; an introduction delivered as if it was nothing really, the most unimportant and boring job in the world. Having seen his photographs of Sienna, Monty said he was minded to "try him out on a small job". It is easy for Neil to remember that specific phrase, not only because of the way it was delivered, but because of its importance to him. "A small job"? It might as well have been the Holy Grail.

Neil finds himself smiling as he sits, retracing the embryonic steps of his professional fortune as it made its journey from the flat in Chalk Farm all the way here, to Parliament Hill, across the best part of a decade and a half. A woman walking her pug happens to glance his way as Neil is mid-memory, and, misinterpreting his expression, chides her dog to walk faster.

The trial had been low cost and low risk. A few days in Edinburgh; first a couple of weeks before the Festival, and then when it was in full-swing.

"I want you to show me what the city's like normally, and then how the Festival transforms it. The Scottishness of it, and then how it becomes something else. International. As if it has been invaded. Make sense? Talk to my PA about arrangements, expenses, that stuff."

Travelling up on the train that July, Neil had reviewed his ideas again, the ones he had been repeatedly sharing with Cath and in the process boring her rigid. Although on the face of it the subject was just another large UK city, it was out of his comfort zone, not the London he knew well, the city he looks at now. Given the nervous uncertainty he had felt then, it might as well have been Tokyo or Timbuktu.

He remembers keeping the pissing dog at the forefront of his mind as he walked Edinburgh's streets that first time. The image had been successful because it had been striking, the dramatic contrast of light and dark; the juxtaposition of the unexpected - the infamous dog! - had given it an edge. Looking through his viewfinder and searching for "Scottishness", he had tried to think 'contrast' and to capture elements - a face, a sign - that perhaps shouldn't have been there. Or should have been left out. He had worried that his plan would backfire. *Condé Nast* was all colour, glitz and beauty; it sold the places it showcased based on their desirability - which wasn't necessarily the first thing his vision would promote. He kept telling himself that Monty had chosen him for a reason, had settled on him based on his black-and-white Campo; if he'd wanted pretty tourist shots he would never have made the call.

Looking out onto the city, he wonders how he would fare now. If Monty were to ring him up and asked him to undertake a similar commission in London, how would that turn out? Not that Neil would take it, of course. He knew the city too well; he was too invested in it; there was too much history. And in any event, he didn't take those kind of photographs any more. Or he hadn't for a long time.

✿

"It's a sign."

Neil turned in his chair, dragging his eyes away from his computer screen and an image of Hampstead Bathing Pond swimmers. He had been trying to crop the photograph to perfect the composition with the aim of then subtly muting the green tones in order to bring out the vibrancy of their bathing costumes and the sparkles of light coming from off the water. Trying and failing. Cath's interruption was a welcome one.

She was sitting on the sofa, an edition of *Condé Nast* - *his* edition of *Condé Nast* - open on her lap.

"What do you mean, 'it's a sign'?"

"This." She nodded to the magazine. "Your article."

Monty had introduced him to Joss Blythe, the person given the job of putting the accompanying words together. Neil and Joss had been able to produce an initial draft quickly enough, to weave a narrative around Neil's photos, but the honing and fine-tuning had taken longer than Neil had expected - and, based on occasional but subtle displays of frustration, possibly longer than Joss was used to. Neil told himself the result was worth the effort.

"It's a little bit surreal, to be honest - seeing my stuff in a magazine like that. But it does prove something doesn't it?"

"What?"

"That I'm okay. Not too shabby - as a photographer, I mean. Just like Charles' exhibition did. This was the next step."

Monty had already indicated there was probably another one to come. He had been impressed enough to float ideas for a second commission. "I like the way you've woven people into the landscape" he said - somewhat pompously, Neil had thought. "I was wondering about doing something outside the UK. Scandinavia, maybe. People in Scandinavia on the edge of Winter, perhaps." They had been at lunch, the arrival of desserts interrupting the flow of the conversation.

"Yes," Cath said, "but that's not what I mean."

"What do you mean then?" Neil had risen from his chair, walked to where Cath sat, and planted himself beside her, easing the open magazine from her lap as he did so. A half-page image of Edinburgh's Royal Mile greeted him, in the foreground, almost creeping out of frame, the entrance to a shop that sold whisky; disappearing into the shop, a customer's trailing leg and the flare of his kilt. If he was honest, he didn't feel the Edinburgh photos really delivered; he knew he could do better. They didn't scream 'Scottishness' as much as he was hoping.

"Everything really." She paused. "The exhibition, the commission, how they came about."

"Your father?"

She nodded.

"And him through me. The flat."

"Opening doors you mean? And in the case of this place, literally so." Neil flicked a page. He couldn't help but reflect that what he had been paid was - perhaps inevitably - less than he had hoped for. He doubted the next commission would offer much more. But that was only to be expected; he was still learning his trade. Perhaps with a few more articles for *Condé Nast* and some work elsewhere, he could increase his fee.

Money was a subject he felt uncomfortable discussing with Cath. He envied her the freedom offered via her father's largesse. She'd never had to worry about things in the way he had, never been subject to the same struggles. They had talked money, of course. Probably prompted by Ralph, she had flat-out asked him what the magazine had paid. They had discussed what that meant, how many more such commissions he might need to secure in order to give up his job. Neil had inflated the fee a little - and deflated the number of contracts he would need to be able to follow his dream. There was always the safety net, of course. Ralph.

Cath tugged the magazine gently to ensure she had his attention.

"You, me, us." She paused again. "Don't you see? How it all fits? How right it is? How right *we* are? Because if it hadn't been, none of this would have happened."

"A sign," he echoed, finally following her logic. It was logic that also led back to Ralph.

He shook himself mentally. He hadn't fallen in love with Ralph, he'd fallen for Cath; her legs, her bravado. Her voice. He didn't believe in 'signs' or in 'fate'; in fact, he wasn't really sure what he believed in. Hard work? Luck? When it came down to it, arriving at a philosophy by which to live his life had never made it to Page One of his day-to-day agenda - not that it seemed to matter. Things were falling into place, he couldn't deny; but that was as far as he went. Clearly there was more in the present sequence of events for Cath; mere happenstance was an insufficient way for her to live her life.

"If I hadn't stopped to talk to you that day on the Heath. If you hadn't taken those photographs of me."

"If you hadn't let me buy you coffee." He tried to play along, but Cath's sudden laughter surprised him; it was as if he had missed the point altogether.

She leant across and kissed his cheek.

"Talking of coffee..." she said, getting up. "Want some?"

Stockholm had been an adventure, though as he recalls it now, looking out over a landscape infinitely more familiar, Neil knows he will never be able to resurrect those initial emotions: landing at the airport, taking the train into the the the city, walking out into a world of unfamiliar signs and where every other girl looked as if she could be a model. It was a romantic reaction, of course, and one he was able to repeat elsewhere and rely on to give him a kick - at least until the novelty of airports and trains began to wear off.

And wear off it did - and more quickly than he might have imagined. The Nordic shoot had been successful enough to earn him a third gig, and - in terms of what he then told himself was far more important - allowed him to produce a couple of decent photographs. Ever since the dog in Siena, he had begun to construct an electronic collection of his best work, partly because he thought that was what he was supposed to do. Never intended as a legacy, it was more the building of a curriculum vitae, a means of answering questions about his experience, a tool to be used in the pitching for work - and something to help justify to both himself and others why he was qualified to follow his chosen profession. That *Condé Nast* used him heavily over the next few months felt at the time like an endorsement of his skills, further independent validation; but after a short period, Neil chose to recognise it as somewhat opportunistic. When that particular light dawned, he knew he had been a cheap resource for the magazine, one who could still be seduced by novelty, travel tickets, and a couple of nights in a half-decent hotel in a new country.

He smiles to himself as his eyes are drawn once again to another aircraft on its glide-path into Heathrow. That had perhaps been his first real awakening as to how the world worked, and of his place in it. Until then everything that had preceded it was little more than foreplay, a phoney understanding of himself. It is not recalling that first instance of awakening which triggers the smile however, but recognising that it was the first of many; harbinger of those other inflexion points which have brought him back to this particular spot on Parliament Hill and on this particular day. Bloodied and bruised from later encounters, he is now preparing himself for another - though in this instance he has no idea how it will go. Checking his watch, Neil registers the minutes left almost as if he was watching a countdown on a map display in a plane flying over the Atlantic: "time to destination". A little under half-an-hour, probably.

A shout nearby draws his attention. Unregistered to that point, a compact game of rounders had been initiated a little way off and a plea to "catch it!" breaks through the background hum as a ball - pursued by a young man in shorts and, somewhat obtusely, an AC-DC t-shirt - comes in his general direction. The ball bounces beyond the fielder, and by the time he finally grabs it, a cheer erupts back at the square as the batter rounds the last base and heads to 'home plate'.

Not that far from here he and Cath had joined in such a game with a few of her work colleagues one Sunday afternoon. Given they were primarily academics rather than athletes, they had proved a motley sporting crew, some of them giving the impression that they were not only new to the game but simultaneously acquainting themselves with running and catching for the first time. Determined to make his mark - and still early enough in his relationship with Cath to deem it necessary to impress her - he had committed himself to an ambitious run round all four bases the first time he was able to launch the ball up the hill. However, not only had he misjudged how far he could hit it, he failed to account for the slope arresting any forward momentum once the ball had landed, and so was run out when well short of his ground. Bravado had prevented him from taking his medicine and stopping at third, the consequence being that he spent much of the rest of the afternoon sitting on the grass watching on with grumpy enthusiasm as Cath and her cronies indulged in a travesty of the game that kept them blissfully entertained for longer than it should have.

The pattern for his daily life post-Stockholm was established well before Neil's enthusiasm for travelling wore off. Drawing his attention back from the present rounders match only to realise he has lost the returning aircraft beneath London's skyline, he tries to travel back in time, to reimagine himself sitting on such a plane, looking out of the window and down on the city as it rises up to meet him. For a while during those early *Condé Nast* days, both ends of his travels had a freshness about them, though anticipation wore thinner more quickly at the domestic end of that particular spectrum. If, in consequence, the younger Neil's landings back in London were tinged with a soupçon of regret he is unable to say. Rather, he prefers to think of those moments as transitions between lives. Had there ever been a time where his life with Cath and his professional pursuits truly overlapped? He struggles to think of one. Perhaps they came closest that day in Siena.

Irrespectively, he likes to look back on that time - he would have been, what, around twenty-five? - with as much fondness as he can muster. Cath had quickly not only established a new routine for them both, but had taken charge of their flat, their domesticity, as if cashing in the chips gifted by her belief in 'the sign'. No matter what he thinks now, Neil knows he could only have been grateful: he was lucky enough to have found himself a beautiful girlfriend - and one with a rich father! - and a new flat to go along with his new career. A further consequence - and almost better than the constituent parts - was that responsibility for a huge chunk of his life was suddenly being taken on by someone else. Although he cannot be certain - this as another shout of "catch it!" accosts him from over his shoulder - perhaps their game of rounders had been such an example: a social event planned and organised by Cath where essentially all he had to do was to turn up and try to play his part.

"Do you realise what a lucky bastard you are?" Harry said to him one evening, the two of them sitting drinking beer in the flat, awaiting the Cath's return from spending the evening with her parents.

"Lucky?"

"All this," Harry gestures to the room. "Nice flat, gorgeous girlfriend, career taking off."

"You forgot to mention the rich father-in-law!"

Harry's laugh is short-lived.

"Indeed. But I wouldn't make a joke of it if I were you."

"Which part?"

"Ralph." Harry paused. "No, I don't mean Ralph, not really."

"So what do you mean?"

"You relationship to him. Cath's father." He looked around the room as if he were checking to see if it had been bugged. "Not that he's your father-in-law. Not yet anyway."

Neil remembers laughing.

"Laugh if you want to, Old Fruit, but I'm telling you, it won't be long before she pops the question..."

"Isn't that my job?" Neil had asked, trying to keep the tone light.

"These days? I'm not so sure. And what if it is? She'll find a way of getting you to, if you'd prefer it that way round..."

Neil can't recall whether he had preferred Harry's revision or not. Indeed, he struggled to remember not only what he had said at that point - some semi-witty retort, he was fairly sure - but also what he may have felt about the idea. Had it come as a revelation to him, a bolt from the blue? Or had Harry merely expressed a notion that he had been wrestling with himself, consciously or otherwise?

Irrespective of that, Harry's words were soon to prove prescient.

Finding himself suddenly in shade, Neil shivers involuntarily and looks up to where a rogue cloud is traversing the sky and blocking out the sun. He watches it move slowly across the blue for as long as he dare, averting his eyes as the sun reaches its boundary, just too late to avoid momentary blinding. Was that how it had been with Cath, the cloud creeping up on him unseen? Or perhaps he was blinded first. If there were clues along the way, he is unable to recall them. Undoubtedly she would have left hints, a breadcrumb trail decipherable by detectives far more intelligent than he. The first he can recall - unbidden exactly as that cloud had been - was triggered by a single word, spoken over a casual dinner at a Pizza Express in Soho. 'Kids' had hit him with the force of a bullet, shot from a rifle with the sniper hiding in plain sight, undisguised by camouflage fatigues.

She had laughed when he echoed her word - *that* he remembers clearly enough! - and reached across the table to take his right hand, his fork paused just above his side-salad.

"Why not?" her tone playful enough for him to be uncertain as to her seriousness. "Not now obviously, but in the future."

"Kids?" For a second time.

"Haven't you ever thought about it? I mean, at some point. Whether or not - one day - you'd like to be a dad?"

He hadn't. And no matter how much she tried to qualify it to an unspecified year into the future, the word was now alive, suddenly between them. Overlooking London with Soho down there somewhere, that very same restaurant buried amongst the

41

rooftops, Neil takes a moment to try and locate it (knowing he will be unable to) as if doing so will either sharpen his memory or distract him from it. He tries to smile, to layer some fondness onto the recollection, to make it benevolent, but is unable to do that either. It occurs to him - perhaps for the first time, unlikely though that may seem - that the pivot points in his life during those few years with Cath were often marked by her adoption of single words which, once unleashed upon him, turned things upside down. 'Sign' had been one, 'kids' another; and he was sure that, if he tried, he might be able to rake through the sludge of his memory to recover more. But what would be the point after all this time? And would the danger not be that he might manufacture invalid examples, torturing himself with too-late recognition of the way points and lay-lines of his life - of *her* life - that he had simply missed? Self-torture is not his objective. Rather than be fixated upon the relationship of those words with his past, surely their value now lay in what they might imply for his future, signposts he now possesses that thirteen years previously he did not. Is that not a definition of wisdom, and is it not wisdom what he will need in about half-an-hour's time?

In spite of Harry's warning, when Cath hit him a few days later with her second blow - an uppercut to follow the jab - Neil was still off-balance. She had said "We should get married, don't you think?" with as unemotional a delivery as she had been able to muster, as if merely the next logical step on the journey, following on from coffee, Ralph, the flat, a 'sign', 'kids'.

He shivers involuntarily again, looking up expecting to see another cloud, but the sky above him is empty. And he realises - surely not for the first time! - that the reason for Cath's mercantile approach had nothing to do with her, but everything to do with him. Knowing her - and knowing what subsequently transpired - how could he have ever thought her unemotional? Oh, she had a way of delivering her messages, using her laughter and her voice - her voice! - to subtle and brilliant effect, but she was the opposite of cold and calculating. Yes, she had inherited some of her father's negotiating traits and they undoubtedly stood her in good stead whenever called upon, but she was as emotionally invested in her life - in *their* lives - as it was possible to be. Despite her often flighty, casual and relaxed approach, in the things that mattered she was never anything other than committed. No. The way in which she had said "We should get married, don't you think?" was all about *him*; she had delivered the line to resonate with her audience.

Was that how she had seen him, Neil wonders. Was that how he was - how he is?

The question is somewhat rhetorical. He knows full-well the answer; indeed, he understands how it will have changed over time. In those early heady days when he was still experimenting with his photography, when Cath was a fresh whirlwind, he could argue that he too was entirely emotional, happy to be taken along for the ride, lacking calculation, blown in whichever direction she wished to take him. Change came, of course, and perhaps one might argue that the stimuli had its origins in 'sign', 'kids' and 'marriage'. That had certainly been Harry's view when he shared it with him later; a view that caused a temporary fissure between them - not because Harry had been wrong, but because he had been right.

Neil closes his eyes for a moment, allowing the sun to warm his eyelids as if the heat will permeate through his body and chase that unwanted shiver away. He concentrates on listening, and allows sound rather than sight to flood his mind, picking out shouts, the odd word from passing conversations, the barks of dogs, and the ever-present hum of the city. And then, satisfied that he has established an appropriate score - a backing track almost - he tries to remember Harry, guilty once again that he was never able to truly heal the partial rift that grew between them. Perhaps he didn't try hard enough. But it is not Harry he sees behind his eyelids, but Cath; Cath sitting on their one armchair across from where he lounged on the sofa, saying "We should get married, don't you think?" but in his own voice not hers. Because ultimately that was what *he* had said - or something akin to it - delivered through an aura of candlelight in another restaurant somewhere, exactly as romantic and non-transactional as it was supposed to be. And she had cried a little and said "yes", and then moved on to other things, as if the word 'marry' had done its job and released others into their shared vocabulary: 'church', 'reception', 'honeymoon'. Neil had felt the spectre of Ralph beside him at the table.

Perhaps ironically, that had been the moment, not recognised until much later - indeed, not until it was entirely too late - where his seismic shift from emotional to transactional had begun.

Because, quite simply, he did not want to marry her.

Had he known it then? Whenever he has asked himself the question - as he inevitably does again now - the answer has always been the same: yes, he had. Yet if that is too definitive, too clear cut, then in an attempt to deal himself a 'get out of jail free' card from the bottom of the pack, he seeks consolation in the mitigation that he hadn't known it in the kind of undeniable, irrevocable, irretrievably self-aware way that brooks no alternative. Rather, it had been an inkling. More than an inkling, if he is honest with himself. Arraigned against Cath's proposal, legions of objections arose, a loosely packed line of defence, each of them powerless on their own and easily swept away; but together?

Equally inept, as it turned out. Neil had marched his troops to the front line individually, partly out of consideration for her and partly because he didn't have the wit or wisdom to get them organised. He wasn't ready for kids, wasn't sure he would be a good father. He drew on deficiencies in his own childhood to suggest the mould from which he was made was flawed. She had disarmed him: "no-one's talking about children *now*" and "you're not your father, are you?". His travelling for *Condé Nast* would somehow get in the way: "is it getting in the way now?"; other observations met with "what difference does that make?". And so the objections evaporated. Other than the simple destruction of everything and walking away from their relationship, he had no killer blow, no one argument that was incapable of being shot down; trotting them out in the way he had was akin to competing against someone at skittles when the target pins were miles away from you but merely an inch from where your opponent was standing.

Before he realised it he was out of ammunition. And yet. And yet.

The more she tried to convince him the more certain he became; but as his certainty grew, his constitution conspired to make him less resolute. In quiet moments he would attempt to regather his strength. He looks away to his left where, out of sight, the path from Gospel Oak wends its way up the hill. He recalls one Sunday afternoon following her as she strode ahead, the two of them attempting to walk off one of her mother's bounteous lunches. In that moment she had seemed as miraculous as ever, as impossible as ever; a wondrous being he had no right to expect would deign to speak to him never mind share their life with him. Tortured by conflicting forces - the desire to grab her so hard that she could never escape, and the urge to turn and flee - he had issued one final battle cry to his forces. They were still there, he could sense them, and he knew that collectively they should have been strong enough to defeat any foe. Or almost any foe. But he had made the fundamental miscalculation in assuming Cath was the one who needed to be vanquished, when all along the fight was with himself. Was it any wonder that she had been able to rebuff his objections so easily? When his troops faced him they seemed a mighty army, and their cries of "no! no! no!" deafening; but when he sent them after her they were inconsequential.

It was on that walk - he could almost pin-point the exact spot, sitting here years later - that he had decided to capitulate. He was tired of the fight, not with Cath but with himself. Naturally he tried to turn his capitulation into something else: he was so lucky; it would be brilliant for him; he loved Cath so much; how would he ever find another like her? They were layers of varnish applied to rotting wood. Eventually the wood shone, but it was still rotten beneath, fragile, and bound to crumble at some future point. This was what Harry had seen but only confessed when it was too late. His "you should never have married her" only merely told Neil what he had known since she had first said "We should get married, don't you think?" - and served to remind him that he had been unable to turn instinct into action. Or inaction, depending on how you chose to view it. He directed his fury at Harry because he had shared his wisdom too late. Why hadn't he been there with him on the battlefield, or was his pronouncement born from the safety and privilege of the hindsight bestowed upon a historian? Yet it became clear later - and has been incontrovertible ever since - that Neil was merely externalising the contempt he felt for himself. He had been a coward. He had taken the easy way out. He had been dishonest.

They had all paid. And now there was a new reckoning coming.

Ahead of him, two children - evidently twins - suddenly appear; they are chasing a small dog that is either making a bid for freedom or is, in turn, playing with them. The dog's barking, the shouts of the children and, from a little way behind, the voice of their mother make up a capsule, a moment destined to be either treasured or forgotten. Instinctively Neil glances down and moves his hand to the bench where he would have expected to encounter his camera bag. If there is any panic in not finding it there it is short-lived. The decision to leave it behind was not taken lightly, but his priority is in not wanting to run the risk of being distracted when Beth is there. He looks back at the children who have already moved to the periphery of his vision and smiles - not at them, but rather at how his Canon (or his many Canons) have become a part of him, as if he is incomplete without them.

He has often wondered if they are better at capturing memory than the mind, or whether what they freeze is something else, something superfluous. If he has become slightly blasé about taking photographs it is because he has taken so many, and because the experience changed significantly when - years before Cath - he acquired his first digital SLR. Prior to that there was a true cost in clicking the shutter: one thirty-sixth of the price of a roll of film; one thirty-sixth of the expense of processing. In those days making a mistake was tangible in more ways than one. Not only that, taking something that was flippant, misguided or might eventually prove irrelevant, occupied a slot in a roll of film, one immediately made unavailable for something else. How many times had a moment presented itself only for him to find that he was at the end of a roll and therefore unable to preserve it? These days he could take shot after shot - six, eight, ten - not needing to worry or aim for perfection first time. It was more likely that the third or fourth in a quickly shot sequence would prove better than the first. Composition rather than accuracy had become king - and he liked to think composition was one of his strengths. His eyes follow the children over the brow of the hill; how many photos would he have taken of them just now? Six? Sixty? In a way the genius in what he does has been moved to a different part of the process, to *after* the photograph is taken, to his big screen and the capability to edit, crop, sharpen, blur. Being a photographer is a different craft to what it had been twenty years before.

Checking his watch and glancing back to the London skyline, he wonders what the photographs of those moments with Cath might have looked like; the moments when she said "We should get married, don't you think?", or when he followed her up the hill from Gospel Oak, his mind changed, him beaten. And what about two years later when he railed against Harry? Those images would have simply shown people walking and talking; the glossy 6x4 would have held none of the context, only silence. Photographs weren't life, he knew that; merely two-dimensional snippets bound by the edges of a rectangle. No matter how much you might want to, you couldn't edit life.

In certain circumstances his photographs held sway over him. Yes, he had invested in high-spec technology - his cameras, computer and software - and yes, he was a skilled practitioner of all the individual elements in the process, but sometimes it was just impossible to turn a bad shot into something worthy. There were times he had spent hours cropping and tinkering, adjusting tints, shadows, highlights, convinced that there was something playing hide-and-seek on the screen waiting to be uncovered. Or discovered. And on far too many occasions the prize had failed to reveal itself. Perhaps it had never been there at all; perhaps he never truly escaped from the belief that every shot he took had the potential to be brilliant if only he could unlock it. Is that photography's most powerful drug? It is his only real sense of professional failure these days: after investing too much time, the moment when he sits back, pushes the mouse and keyboard away, and finds himself staring at something he simply doesn't recognise any longer - not the image itself, but the moment it had strived to capture. The seriousness, the humour, the action he had seen and tried to grasp has vanished. On such occasions, all he is left with is a mess, a pastiche, and the only recourse when that happened was to throw the thing away. Hit the delete button.

No, you couldn't edit life.

❈

"You won't let your dad go over the top, will you?"

Although framed as a question, the words had escaped from him more in the manner of a plea than anything else.

"What do you mean?"

They had been spending the evening planning. It seemed to Neil that was how most of their evenings were now spent: Cath home from work, the dinner he had prepared, a usually disappointing half-an-hour spent watching the television, then she would turn the conversation toward matrimonial matters. When he wasn't away on an assignment for *Condé Nast* (perhaps three or four days a month), spending the day editing and honing, or undertaking speculative visits to potential shooting locations, he had time to be 'domestic'. He liked to call his excursions 'projects'. As his electronic library of these had grown - impromptu shots of tourists at the Tower of London, stallholders at Leadenhall Market, commuters at Victoria station - the criticality of his computer (now a Mac) had increased, and he spent a disproportionate amount of his time at his desk securing multiple back-up copies of his images. The non-*Condé Nast* contracts were a rag-bag of opportunities: the odd piece of work for a Sunday supplement, a sporting event, even political rallies. Although he was becoming known in a marginal way, his coterie was still too small, his income too meagre, his self-esteem too low. Neil felt diminished when it came to their upcoming wedding too; Cath was in the driving seat, in charge of everything that would be seen and tasted. And - all too often, it seemed - also in charge of what would be felt. In the background her father lurked; a person of influence.

"You know. You're his only daughter; it's only natural he might want to push the boat out, make it memorable."

She laughed.

"Shouldn't it be memorable?"

"You know what I mean," he replied, unsure of his ground. "I want it to be intimate rather than grand, personal and not public. Does that make sense? I have this image of some huge church where your side is packed to the rafters and I have to drag people in off the street to even half-fill my side."

"Well the church isn't going to be huge," Cath said definitively, ignoring the joke. "You remember our shortlist? We've settled on St Helen's, Bishopsgate. The restoration work after the bombing is marvellous, and it seems a perfect way to celebrate both us and the church."

Neil noted how she said 'we've' - and how that 'we' didn't include him.

On one level he didn't mind; indeed he was quite grateful that the burden of decision-making rested elsewhere. Moreover, he trusted Ralph's taste, and was as sure as he could be that his guiding hand and influence over Cath would be nothing but beneficial. Yet there was still an underlying discomfort. Not only was he facing into something over which he had limited control, it was a journey he privately remained unconvinced he wanted to take.

"Of course I will," Harry had said when Neil had proposed he be his Best Man, "who else are you going to get to do it?!"

"If only Sean Connery had been available," Neil joked.

"Now he would have been a bad choice!"

"How so?"

"Probably run off with all the bridesmaids, and Cath too!"

They had laughed appropriately. Neil was pleased Harry seemed up for the challenge; he felt he needed an ally.

How many more allies he might have in attendance on the day itself was open to question. He and Cath had settled on numbers:

numbers in the church, numbers for the reception, numbers for the party in the evening. Having no choice but to go along with them, although not vast, Neil remained daunted by their scale. He wasn't sure he knew fifty people, never mind a hundred or more. When they started to compile lists, Cath raced through hers adding names of aunts, uncles, cousins he had never heard of; even having dredged up semi-ostracised branches of his mother's family, for Neil getting beyond thirty was problematic.

"I'll lend you some of mine," Cath had said, "just to balance up the church."

It *had* been wonderful, of course. A spectacle stage-managed to within an inch of its life, every element going like clockwork. Throughout the day people had told him where to be, what to do, what to say; it was as if he had been dropped into a play at the last minute, an extra whose contribution was later commended as 'flawless' - though not because of anything he added to proceedings. Indeed, the whole thing had been memorable, just as Cath had predicted: the church was just the right size; some of her guests bled to his side to give the impression of balance; the reception had been splendid with Ralph and then Harry stars of the show. Neil had no doubt that Cath's father would be able to command a room, something he did with aplomb and subtlety, but Harry had been a revelation; Neil suspected there had been more crying over his borderline jokes than tears of joy at the ceremony itself.

If anything was ever inevitable, however, it was that Neil would end up dissatisfied with the wedding photographs. Nestling on the bottom shelf of the bookcase in the spare bedroom were the two leather-bound volumes which had been presented to them on their return from honeymoon. Sitting on the bench, uncrossing his legs to avoid pins-and-needles, the frustration he felt when he first flicked through them has moderated a little with the passing of time. But it is still there. They were typically unimaginative shots of the bride-and-groom, wedding family 'A', wedding family 'B'; with the groom, without the groom. He could have made an educated guess before the event at what was to be included and been ninety-plus precent accurate in his forecast. Because of the adherence of 'Fletcher and Bow, Specialist Wedding Photographers' to their standard template, Neil had subsequently come to feel he could have been looking at anybody's wedding - a sensation that never left him in spite of his not retrieving the albums from their resting place in an awfully long time. Or not until yesterday. More preparation and context. But that old frustration, newly rekindled perhaps, was not merely about content; their execution bothered him, primarily because they weren't his photos.

Cath had made him promise he wouldn't take his camera to the church or reception: "I don't want to see it until we get off the plane" she had said. Her argument had been that it was their special day and so he should regard it as a holiday from his camera. "Let someone else have that worry" she said, not realising that for him *not* having a camera to hand would be the source of an even greater concern. Although ostensibly he had complied, his doing so was at best superficial; secreted in the inner pocket of his hired wedding suit was a small 'instant', later transferred to the more casual jacket he wore to the party afterwards. Surreptitiously, like a Cold War spy, he had been able to extract it from time-to-time to capture something about the day that was - to his eye - more authentic. If Cath had spotted him as he slipped to the periphery of things during those moments, either outside the church or beyond the dance-floor, moments when his physical presence had not been demanded and he could retrieve the Olympus from his pocket - snap, snap - she never said. The outcome of this renegade activity was a small collection, eventually suitably catalogued on his Mac, of smartly dressed people caught off-guard; moments when they weren't adopting their best smiles to accompany a formal pose or a request to 'smile please!'. Individually they said more about the people present than the 'official' images ever could: Ralph constantly on his mettle, never wavering in his role of the proud father; Cath gloriously resplendent except in one picture when she is talking to an old school friend who had just been diagnosed with MS; his aunt and uncle standing a little too far apart, always looking in opposite directions, and who would be divorced within the month. The one person who he had most interest in seeing, guard down, was himself; but he was only to be discovered suitably bound in the leather volumes, officially smiling.

For her part, Cath seemed to be everywhere; the centre of everything, the flame to which all the other guests were drawn. When he had looked at the albums yesterday, sitting on the spare bed rather than removing them from their place of exile, he could not help but be reminded how astonishing she had been. Without doubt the day had belonged to her. It hadn't really been their wedding, it had been *hers* - and perhaps that was at the heart of the problem. He told himself he didn't mind that his part in the day had somehow been tangental, that he hadn't minded then and didn't now. Indeed, it seemed right and proper, looking back all these years later, that she should have had her moment in the sun even though no-one knew exactly what it meant nor what would follow. In a way the photographs represented transition, the moment when responsibility for what had happened and what was to happen transferred between them. Although Cath's subsequent actions had been hers alone, he could not escape the fact that he had been the agent provocateur.

From the outset - even from those words "We should get married, don't you think?" - there was little doubt she had staked everything on that gambit. Sitting in the sun, watching passers-by in a vague and detached way, Neil likens that moment to someone putting all their chips on black then standing back, not in hope, but in the certain knowledge that the small silver ball will land in two, four, six, eight, ten, eleven or some such. Cath hadn't been prepared for it to nestle in red. Or perhaps more alarmingly for them both, in zero; no-one winning. And to be frank, neither had he. She had been the first real whirlwind in his life, and had scooped him up to carry him careering through time. It had been a ride he had only come to appreciate seven years later - three years later than he had needed to. He glances back up the hill to the spot they first met, imagines himself lying on the grass, camera to his eye, trying to frame London. Detached both from himself and time, he sees her approach, crouch down beside him, hears those first words, watches again the way she posed for him. And he is unable to reconcile that free spirit with the Cath she became once they were married: still beautiful, lively, vivacious; still a mystery to him; but suddenly no longer a girl but a woman, married not to him but to the role of being married; a woman who had - to his mind at least - embarked on a crusade, a new role that would demand she sweep all before her. Him included. Yet even as he thinks that, he knows it is only partially true, that to characterise her attitude to the next stage of their life together in such a way is unfair; he knows he had an equal role to play - not in their marriage, but in its outcome. And it is important he recognises that truth today. Preparation and context. Because there is another whirlwind in the air.

Two

"Have you ever thought of trying other sorts of work?"

Rico had approached him stealthily. Even though the gallery picked up every sound and amplified it, Neil failed to register his presence until he spoke. It was a voice which belied its inherently smooth and silky tone by cutting through the background hubbub of chatter and the clinking of glasses. Although it was his second appearance in the annual *Condé Nast* photography exhibition, Neil had yet to decide if he liked the event. The previous year, still being a new boy, they had shown just three of his Edinburgh photographs, tucked away in a relatively remote corner destined to see less footfall than anywhere else. This time not only had these been reprised - and with the inclusion of the kilted-man entering the wine shop! - they had been supplemented with three of his Scandinavian winter shots, plus a selection from other assignments: Dubrovnik, Barcelona, Paris, Cannes during the film festival. Neil had been particularly pleased with the latter. More homage to the place than the event, he had managed to capture some A-listers at the very edges of photographs as if they were the least important component, photobombing rather than centre stage.

At first glance Neil found the man standing next to him almost a caricature. Everything about him was impeccable: the cut of his suit, the blend of shirt and tie, the shine on his shoes, the precision of his small goatee.

"Other sorts of work?"

Rico extended a perfectly manicured hand. As Neil took it he sensed it belonged to either a showman or someone who was incredibly wealthy.

"Rico," the man smiled, as if a christian name was sufficient. "Yes, other sorts of work. I mean, you clearly have an exceptional eye: composition, detail, juxtaposition, colour. But what am I saying? You wouldn't be working for *Condé* if you weren't any good!"

He laughed at his own joke, showing his perfect teeth.

"I'm always open to opportunities," Neil admitted, playing the only 'come and get me' card he had. Yes, he was getting a steady flow of work through the magazine, but it was hardly sufficient to meet either financial needs or professional ambition, and additional contracts were all too sporadic and proving difficult to acquire. He and Cath were not under any real pressure financially - indeed, with Ralph in the background how could they be? - but a desire for them to be truly independent always hovered somewhere, nagging at him. Cath had been talking again about children, something Neil felt incompatible with both his income and their flat.

"People," Rico charmed, turning his attention to the display in front of them. "You have a knack, I think. That's where your true talent lies." He raised an arm and extended an index finger; it was a gesture laden with expression. "Look. This one in Stockholm with the couple at the sauna; and these two in Cannes, especially the one where you've deliberately omitted half of Julia Roberts! And the Barcelona ones, especially La Barceloneta, down on the beach."

Neil followed the finger as it pointed.

"But some of those, well, anyone could have taken them." His protest, claiming modesty, was a weak one.

"Perhaps. Perhaps not. But *you* did. And do you know what's so remarkable about them?"

"Tell me." Neil had smiled, not realising he was already hooked.

"Trust," said Rico, turning back to him. It was as if, in the way he said it, he oozed the word rather than spoke it, subconsciously and simultaneously proposing to Neil that he trust him too. Indeed, the voice seemed to be demanding how could he not?

"Trust?"

"Here," Rico turned and pointed again, still smiling but a little more in earnest. "These two women on the beach in Spain; the same in Cannes, the way that one is staring straight into your camera, smiling; that lady at the market stall in Dubrovnik. People don't interact with a camera, they respond to the photographer. I know there's a theory that some just turn it on when they see a lens - your Cannes A-listers probably, they're professionals after all - but normal people? I don't think so. Most are suspicious of people they don't know wielding cameras - especially men with cameras! I look at some of these and see nothing but trust. Add that to your other more obvious talents... Well, that's quite a cocktail."

As was Rico's flattery. Neil did not considered himself especially vain, but it was difficult for him not to accept the compliment as gospel, even if he still had no idea where it might be leading.

"Thanks. That's very nice of you."

"So," said Rico, turning his back on the photographs as if they had served their purpose and now facing Neil square on, "back to my original question: have you thought of other sorts of work? Work that would utilise all your skills."

Having laid sufficient emphasis on the word 'all', Neil could see Rico was making it perfectly plain that he was drawing a direct line between work and this new attribute, 'trust'.

"Such as?"

"People, as I said. Oh, you can make a place look nice - colourful, attractive, alluring - but so can dozens of others. Hundreds. Because a place is just a place, never open to moods, emotional swings; all you need is the right light, the building never changes." Sensing Neil was about to object, Rico raised a hand. "But *people* constantly change, minute by minute, second by second. Yes, you need the right light and all that, but you need to build relationships with them in order to be a great photographer."

"Trust?"

"Exactly! Combining *all* your skills, I think you could be exceptional at making people look good. Who wouldn't want to go to Dubrovnik having seen some of your photographs? Well, the trick is to achieve the same reaction with people: who wouldn't want to know that person, wear those clothes, try that make-up? I think you could lift people up and make them extraordinary, just as you did in Spain or Sweden."

If Neil had been expecting something to follow, an immediate extension to Rico's assertion, he was disappointed. The other man paused, clearly giving the cue that it was now his turn to speak. Years later - sitting on a bench on Parliament Hill - Neil reflects again on how he had missed the line tighten, the hook embedded more firmly in his mouth, Rico about to make the final strike.

"And would it be that you have - I'm not sure what the right word is - contacts in this area, or some influence perhaps?"

Rico laughed, a silverly slippery kind of laugh that glistened from him.

"My dear young man, I'm offering you some work!"

✿

Even now, after all that has happened, there is still a part of Neil that retains a fondness for the man. Replaying their first meeting as he does now - simultaneously debating whether or not it is warm enough to remove his jacket - he has no doubt that if, at that precise moment, Rico had suddenly appeared, he would have been unable not to welcome him.

But that is not merely unlikely to happen, it is impossible. Since Neil had severed his professional relationship with him (just a few years after their first meeting) the truth broke, an accumulation of rumour finally morphing into fact - or close enough to fact to see Rico shifted to the wrong side of the law, falling off the tightrope it transpired he had been walking for a considerable period of time. Not that Neil had been surprised at the news - nor that it had come from Beth. Given the extremes their relationship ended up touching and the less salubrious offerings of Rico's 'portfolio' to which he had succumbed for a while, it could hardly be otherwise. Instinctively Neil glances to the south-west, approximately to where Wormwood Scrubs sits, invisibly nestling down beyond Kilburn and Kensal Green. Rico had only been held there a short while before his trial, a sojourn subsequently followed by a similarly short-term incarceration in Ford open prison from where it was no journey at all to the ferries of the south coast. The evidence against Rico had proved typically slippery and thus insufficient for any higher category detention, and the rumours which gathered about him prior to his arraignment, like moths to a flame, were followed by others after his release: he had gone to live in France, or Spain, or he had returned to an ancestral family seat in Italy - with the emphasis on 'family'. Neil had no interest in believing any of them, although he was as certain as he could be that Rico had conclusively given up on the UK - and that he had been a

59

shrewd enough operator to have sequestered funds in multiple locations as insurance against his past one day catching up with him.

Harry had met him once, a brief encounter during that period when the elastic which joined he and Neil was stretching dangerously close to breaking point - and when Neil was on the slide himself, making the transition from one kind of life to another. "He's a slime-ball," had been Harry's considered verdict, and though Neil can now see the veracity in his pub-grade assessment - indeed, has seen it for a while - he still feels it too superficial. In his own mind Rico was a complex character, and in some aspects diametrically opposed to what many thought. Or most, in fact.

Neil's initial job had been innocent enough.

"I have a contact in the Rag Trade who needs a photoshoot of their upcoming Spring range. They're no-one particularly special - I mean, not a big High Street name - but there you are. I've access to a small studio, lighting and a lighting guy, and I have contacts in terms of models... All I now need is someone talented to press the shutter."

Unsure what he had expected, even now Neil is unable to rationalise the reaction he must have had. Although he had no clue as to Rico's 'trade' - and remained oblivious to the underlying nature of it for a few months - all these years later he can only assume he must have felt an initial disappointment at such a low-key opportunity. It was, Rico had suggested, "just a start", "to try you out", "to see if you like it". He had dangled the carrot of other projects he had in mind: more artistic scope, vaguely 'larger' shoots. "Right up your street". If he had wavered at any point, the fee - twice *Condé Nast*'s hourly rate - sealed the deal.

Neil recalls Cath's ambivalence. By that point they had been married for over a year, and, having established their new norm, were both already looking to change it, though in different directions - not that he recognised it then as clearly as he does now, hindsight providing a more educated overlay on their lives together. He wonders if the years have inadvertently allowed him to varnish their past, not in order to make it shine but rather to fix it in place. In one way or another, impatience categorised both of them: Neil desperate to move on beyond the magazine, Cath to build an enlarged family unit. All the things he felt at the time, Neil now recognises as half-formed; emotions and desires defined by instinct and without wisdom. The latter is something he now feels he possesses in spades - and which he has earned, paying his dues across the intervening years. Whether it is that same wisdom which allows him to sit on a bench on Parliament Hill and scan the city, to take-in the people nearby, that permits him to make assessments and judgements, to know when to press the shutter or to be more patient, he cannot say for certain. Though there must be a connection. Back then it would have been easy to have given in again, to acquiesce to Cath's wish for a family; but something stopped him. He rationalised it as an incompatibility - not with her or her idea, but with his vision of himself slowly emerging from the fog. This time, the more he resisted, the more she pushed; the more she pushed, the more he held firm. Perhaps the alarm bells should have rung more loudly the day it occurred to him that, whatever he felt or wanted, he was entirely in her hands: on a practical level not only was he relying on Cath for their financial safety net (via Ralph, of course!), but more pertinently for birth control, and without telling him she could have unilaterally chosen to stop taking the pill at any moment.

Given such a background - and what soon enough became a domestic unravelling - Rico's proposal shone like a beacon.

Now established as a binary choice, he has asked himself many times what would have happened had he not accepted Rico's offer and instead given in to Cath. He does so again now as he sits and waits. The outcome of his deliberations is always the same: he doesn't know. Not because he doesn't have the wit to imagine the new life they would have had - the move to a house in the suburbs, the family car, the school run - but because the varnish he has applied to his past is too thick. It has become an immutable seal, there to protect himself as much as anything else.

The 'rag trade' shoot had been straightforward but ostensibly dull. The first press of the shutter allowed him to overcome the almost schoolboy-like excitement of working in a studio with proper ancillary equipment - not to mention a lighting guy! It was as if making the commitment to an initial exposure flicked a switch. Even the novelty of working with a real live model, one who was entirely at his beck and call, quickly lost its lustre. He found himself going about his business, trying to focus on making the clothes look good even if a range of largely floral-print dresses was not a subject he would have chosen for himself. He tries to recall the frisson he felt when he got back to the flat from the shoot, buzzing with the sensation that he had just taken another step on the ladder; but he can only remember Cath being particularly belligerent that evening, seeming to belittle his work, pressing him hard with the conviction that it was essentially irrelevant compared to what she wanted for them. Up until that point they had never argued. He remembers going from elated to deflated in a heartbeat, from triumphant to the verge of defeat. They ate dinner in virtual silence and then Neil rang Harry to see if he fancied a drink.

✧

"Tough day?"

Harry had broken the silence.

"No, great day really; it's just the last couple of hours that haven't been up to much."

"Well," said Harry, clearly a little confused, "you don't look as if you've had a great day."

There was a pause Neil declined to fill.

"So how was the voluptuous model?"

"Not so voluptuous." The question forced Neil to smile. "Chlöe. Perfectly pleasant; thin as a rake. According to the lighting man, Ray, exactly the shape needed to make the clothes look good."

"And did they?"

Neil shook his head.

"Don't ask me; I'm no expert in knee-length floral print dresses."

"But you must have a view."

"Sure. They looked nice enough on Chlöe. Suited her, I suppose. She was pretty in a mid-counties kind of way; would have looked good in a riding outfit, that kind of thing. But accent as coarse as they come. Not that we talked much. Between shots, while she was changing, over coffee."

"And what about you?"

"Me?" It was Neil's turn to look perplexed.

"Taking those kind of photos; being in a studio. How did it feel?"

Neil rummaged for a response, trying to drag himself back to earlier in the day.

"Good, I guess. Different. Exciting, I suppose. I was a bit nervous, but once we got started… By the end of the session it all seemed natural enough, the studio, the lighting, the model."

"So a good thing, right?" Harry tried to make the question sound upbeat. Neil nods. "So why the long face? You've just finished your first shoot with a proper model and all the rest of it, and your friend Rico has indicated that, provided you haven't cocked it up, there will be more; yet in spite of all that, you look like the guy who's lost a tenner and found a fiver."

Neil looked down into his glass, the head from his pint having thinned to be almost non-existent. It seemed representative of something, but he wasn't sure what.

"It's Cath." He answered without looking up.

"Oh." Harry examined his own beer and waited.

"I get home all fired-up about my day and all she can talk about is family, kids, as if what I've done isn't important, as if it doesn't matter."

"Well maybe it isn't."

"What?"

"Important to her. Or certainly not as important as her wanting kids. Clock ticking and all that."

"I understand all that," Neil sighed and looks up, "but it's getting more - I don't know - oppressive. It's the only thing she talks about. I feel like she's trying to paint me into a corner."

"Again."

As soon as the word was out it was clear from the way his face flushed slightly that Harry regretted it. He glanced at Neil then averted his eyes, returning to his glass which he lifted from the table with exaggerated deliberation, forlornly hoping if he did so slowly and carefully enough the word would somehow be forgotten.

"Again?"

❖

"How do you feel about a calendar shoot?"

Neil looks across the hill at the trees, up at the sky, the vague shimmer off the city, and wonders how accurately he is able to locate a place in time. After all the thousands of photographs he has taken across the years, he would like to think he has some sense of such things. The trees have that rich green tone which means it is no longer early spring nor late enough for some of them to be thinking of turning; the sky, however, lacks the depth of blue you can get in high summer which confirms June rather than July or early August. But English weather is an unreliable and deceptive thing. He could be sitting here in April or October and the meteorological similarities with today - sunshine, heat - prove comparable. He remembers the cold Nordic shoot; the weather there, he was told, was as reliable as clockwork - especially in terms of temperature.

Neil had instinctively transferred Rico's words into a vision of a long-term project spread out across the months, translated them into an anathema of chocolate-box villages or jigsaw-ready images of National Trust properties swathed in snowdrops or bluebells, daffodils or roses. When he had frowned, the other man had laughed. It wasn't that kind of calendar shoot Rico was suggesting.

Rico's rag trade client had been pleased with what Neil had delivered and selected some twenty or thirty images of Chlöe showing off a representative range of dresses which he would combine into a small promotional booklet to be mailed out to a potential customer list procured through a marketing agency. On the inside back cover, adjacent to the form buyers could complete, an acknowledgement in very small print: "photographs by...".

It had been something of an anti-climax. As Neil watches people variously enjoying the mid-June weather, he recalls how disappointed he had been; his contribution seemed of scant import, almost irrelevant, worthless. He had wanted to be more than a mere contributor, a bit-part player on a scrawny mini-catalogue. It was hardly getting his name in lights! Ten years on, now that he has achieved his goal - or a derivative of it with which that early version of himself would surely be satisfied - he is reminded just how naïve he had been back then about 'fame', and how flimsy such recognition was.

Rico had been true to his word. After the floral dresses there had been three other small jobs: promotional shots of a newly modernised hotel for their brochure and website; a day at Goodwood's 'Festival of Speed' when Rico happened to be there racing a Porsche; and more retail work, though this time contributing to a catalogue for shoes - with, it seemed to Neil at the time, more emphasis on the girls' legs than the shoes themselves. Rico had a finger in all three of those particular pies. His Porsche was resplendent in gleaming metallic black, and he later confessed to having made "a small investment" with an old acquaintance in the hotel concerned. And the shoes? Well, it later transpired it *was* more about the legs than the leather. Still, he proved easy to work for, giving Neil as much control as he wanted over the mechanics of each shoot - as long as he adhered to the brief. And he paid well. The money had been especially welcome, not merely to endorse Neil's chosen career path and demonstrate in very real terms that he was making progress, but because it allowed him to relax a little, removing some of the financial pressure he felt, imagined or otherwise. Whether he knew it or not at the time, the extra income helped nudge Ralph a little further back in his consciousness.

"I have an acquaintance in the building supplies trade," Rico continued, "who likes to send his customers a calendar every year, the sort of thing that shows off his products: hard hats, high-vis, boots, tool belts. He is, I suppose, what you might call 'a traditionalist', but he knows his market. And he knows his customers. They are, you might say, at the more 'agricultural' end of the spectrum. So his calendars tend not to be particularly politically correct, if I may use that phrase." He paused for a moment. "Do you get the picture, Neil?"

Indeed he did. Rico was describing a calendar you might see on the wall of a building-site Portakabin or in the back office of builders' merchants - though undoubtedly less so now than once upon a time.

"I have no idea what it must be like working in those kinds of environments," Rico continued without waiting for a firm response, "but I suppose the odd diversion is welcome. In any event, he's asked me if I could produce next year's calendar for him (I sourced one a couple or three years ago), and so, not unnaturally, I thought of you."

"Me?" Rico's last phrase trumped the objection Neil was about to raise.

"Of course." He smiled. "Not only has what you've done for me thus far been top drawer, you've got on well with the models, which is vital. It's that 'trust' Neil, like I said before. Indeed, one or two of them have said how much they'd like to work with you again."

"Really?"

"Claire and Amanda from the shoe brochure, and Chlöe from the dress catalogue - though I don't think she'd be quite right for this job."

"Oh?"

Rico tried to look uncomfortable.

"Doesn't have quite the right 'attributes', if you get my drift." Again he didn't pause for a response. "We'd use the same studio as before I think - maybe even one or two 'on location' shots, if you think that would be appropriate. And Ray for the lighting, of course. What do you think?"

His instinct was to decline. It wasn't as if there was anything intrinsically wrong with what he'd done for Rico to-date, but a builders' calendar hardly seemed the next logical step in the direction he had imagined his career taking. And he wasn't sure Cath would approve. As he was formulating a sentence in his head that would allow him to say 'no', Rico applied the coup de grâce.

"We're all set-up to start next week. And it's worth three times the shoe job to you - for just a couple of days' work."

Neil was hooked again.

"No shit!" said Harry that evening when they were in the pub.

"No shit," Neil confirmed. "Monday, at that loft studio place we used before down near the river."

"You lucky…"

"Yes, I know: lucky bastard."

"But you don't seem that excited, Old Fruit. I mean, what's not to like; taking photos of girls just wearing a donkey jacket and a smile!"

Neil couldn't help but grin.

"Every boy's dream, right?"

"Beats a train set every time! So how does it work? I mean, have they told you exactly what they want; Miranda bent over a cement mixer, something like that?!"

They both laughed.

"Not really. There's a range of products that I have to include in at least one of the final photos, but exactly how I do that is down to me and the models. They've given me the last couple of years' calendars as an example of what they're after. And I get the impression that one or two of the girls may have done this kind of thing before. At least I hope so."

Harry shook his head, still smiling.

"I think I may have to take up photography."

As he had expected, Cath hadn't been that impressed with the new commission - but not in the sense of disapproving of his taking on the work. He had told Harry first in order to gauge the merits or demerits of his decision before he broke the news to her. Harry's predictable enthusiasm hadn't helped provide him with a balanced view. Looking at it dispassionately, the prospect of selling her what could only be regarded as a 'dodgy' job proved too daunting, and so the following day he found himself painting a more impressionistic picture of the contract, utilising an exceedingly limited range of words to describe it and choosing to avoid any that might refer, directly or indirectly, to its 'coarser' elements. What saved him from embarrassment and objection were her own preoccupations, and - from his interpretation of her response - a growing disinterest with what he was trying to achieve.

Reflecting on it once again, he wonders if he is able to trace that degeneration back to his early *Condé Nast* days, if not all the way to those photographs in Siena. Indeed, perhaps she had only ever been truly interested once, here on Parliament Hill, the day they met; yet even then her agenda was entirely her own. If he were to assess Cath's engagement with his work for *Condé*, the nine-out-of-ten he would have scored it in relation to his Edinburgh shoot was soon enough relegated to a seven when it came to Barcelona, and by the time Rico appeared on the scene it was a five at best. It had been supplanted in turn by their engagement, the wedding, and then her unswerving commitment to the future she was trying to construct for both of them; it was as if Cath had discovered a limit in her capacity for enthusiasm, and when her primary focus needed more, something else had to give. As he sees it now - full of their histories, engaging the city below in an abstract dialogue - her growing disinterest had been the most concrete evidence of the divergent paths they had started to take as soon as she had said "We should get married, don't you think?".

Did he feel at all liberated by her apparent lack of engagement? He honestly believes he did not. Rather, it was another concern to be added to a growing list about which he should have been increasingly worried. "But", the city seems to counter as he stares at it, the voice he bestows upon it inevitably Harry's, "back then you couldn't possibly have known what it all implied; how could you? Everything was a natural progression, the process of working things out. You'd never been in that position before, so don't crucify yourself because of an absurd notion that you should have known or that you could have done something about it." Things were to get worse before they got better. "Worse", concurs the city, "definitely worse."

❖

The first day of the shoot did not go well, initial troubles with the lighting rig and the delays to which that led proving prescient. Neil struggled with both composition and his models, the latter never quite seeming to grasp what he was trying to achieve. He was aware of Claire and Amanda sitting in a corner whispering while they smoked, waiting for he and Ray to set-up the next shot; it felt as if any goodwill he had earned with them on the shoe contract had evaporated. Each time he framed the girls he tried to think like a builder, tap into some basic manly instinct, to visualise what he would have expected - or wanted! - to see in March, April, May. But he found he could only think like a photographer. Perhaps he was also discomforted by how unselfconscious they were when in front of the camera, and he envied Ray's detachment, his air of 'been there, done that'. Naïvety and the fact that it *wasn't* water off a duck's back for him were the biggest issues. When they wrapped up early, they did so with everyone in a pretty foul mood and their plan to have captured at least five months' worth of shots lying in tatters. Cath's prior arrangement to spend the evening at her parents saved Neil an uncomfortable cross-examination when he got home.

It was Claire who saved the shoot. When Neil arrived at the studio the following morning, she and Amanda were already there and had been joined by a younger model, Sam. His attempt at a cheery "good morning" was met, not in similar vein, but with the three woman walking in concert to the middle of the studio and standing full square in front of him. For a moment he was reminded of scenes from classic Westerns, just before the good guys and bad guys engage in the climactic shoot-out.

"Look Neil, we can't have another day like yesterday," said Claire, adopting the tone of spokesperson. Ray, who had been repositioning some spotlights, stopped doing so; it appeared this might be worth his attention.

"I agree," Neil said.

"So, here's the thing," Claire pushed on before Neil could add anything further. "We've done this sort of thing dozens of times - well, me and Mandy anyway. Sam's relatively new to it, aren't you?"

"Only my third," Sam confirmed, refraining from elaborating further.

"You're very sweet, and you're clearly trying to do what you think's right and all, but at the end of the day this is just a smutty calendar, Love. It's not high art."

Neil glanced at Ray who, standing slightly behind him, had chuckled at this.

"So we just need to reset," Claire continued. "We know what the punters want." She nodded to the other girls and in unison all three dropped the robes they had been wearing. They were completely naked. "This is us, and this is what they want. The vests and other stuff's just for titillation, really; an excuse. The calendar's not about all that product bullshit. The guys who hang these calendars on their walls don't give a damn about high-vis or big boots."

"Big boobs, more like," Amanda interjected, at which they all laughed. Neil felt a bubble of tension burst.

"So take a long hard look, Neil. At us. Your job, Love, is *not* to make the products look good, but to make *us* look good. Better than good. Remember the shoe thing? Never about the shoes, was it? Always about us, about our legs. Well this is the same - except they want to see a bit of boob and a tease elsewhere."

There was a pause, one only broken when Neil realised that they expected him to speak - and that he had indeed been looking at the three of them, taking them all in, admiring how they were, comparing the shape and size of their breasts, their legs, their hips.

"I..." he hesitated, realising he was blushing as if he'd been caught with his hand in the cookie jar. Everyone laughed again.

"Do you get it?" Amanda asked, her tone slightly softer than Claire's.

Neil nodded.

"Absolutely. And of course, I should have no trouble at all in making the three of you look stunning."

And he didn't. More than that, by the end of what proved to be a stimulating and energetic day, Neil began to feel a little like a builder himself.

"I've seen the proofs," Rico said when he called him the following week. "Absolutely super, spot on. There's no way Jim won't like them. Better than last year's by a mile."

"I can't take all the credit," Neil confessed.

"Oh?"

"The girls. Very" - Neil search for the word - "professional."

The other man laughed.

"Yes, you might say that. Not their first rodeo, as our American cousins would say. But it's not just about them is it? I mean, team effort and all that. They're only that - professional - when they have a rapport with the guy holding the camera. It's what I said at the very beginning, Neil."

"Trust," Neil said, just to prove that he had been paying attention.

✿

Interrogating the skyline's landmarks, Neil tries to call to mind the calendar in detail. But he can only picture April - Claire, one foot on the bottom rung of a stepladder, large spirit level strategically placed, her high-vis indiscreetly unfastened - and August - a jacketed Claire again, this time bent over set of architect's drawings, hard-hatted, wearing a tool-belt around her waist and a look of concentration. He had asked for one copy from the production run which, in turn, he had given to Harry - if only to hear again the confirmation that he was a 'lucky bastard'. And on numerous levels he knew he was. It seemed as if he was going to be able to make a go of his chosen career, a prize he knew eluded the majority - assuming they had an inkling as to what they wanted to do in the first place! Not only that, doing so had exposed him to the kind of situation which most men would give their eye-teeth to experience: not just the two days with a selection of attractive young women who were near-naked most of the time, but the Condé Nast travelling, being paid to experience other places and other cultures. Had there been a tally, Neil knew the column of positives would have been more heavily populated that its counterpart.

Yet there were also things that had worried him, things he wasn't sure he recognised at the time and about which - given the events that followed - he has often cross-examined himself. Of course everything relating to Cath was to come under an intense spotlight within two years of the calendar shoot, a spotlight shone not only by him but *on* him too. Should he have been more concerned that she didn't once ask to see the calendar? If her continuing and deepening disinterest in his work had rung alarm bells, why didn't he hear them? And if he did, faint or not, why did he choose to ignore them? Or if he didn't ignore them, why didn't he act in a different way, a 'better' way? The foundation for many of these queries originated with Ralph long before he adopted the radio silence that has existed between them ever since.

A couple - middle-aged, well-dressed - pause a few yards in front of him to take in the view, partly obscuring his own. The man points, first south-east and then his arm arcs towards the west; it seems the logical progression. He looks like the kind of person - professional, intelligent - who should be able to answer Neil's questions, and for a bizarre moment he has a desire to sit them down next to him, to relate his entire story and then seek answers, as if their responses would somehow be definitive. He smiles at his foolishness, and then almost simultaneously realises (as if for the first time, though it is not) that he *has* people who can help him to reach a conclusion. Harry is obviously one, but to get back to how they were all those years ago when he met Cath for the first time still requires something undefinable from them both; in consequence, Neil fears Harry is not the reliable witness he once was. No more than he is himself, of course. As the couple move away - the man glancing to where Neil sits, an imperceptible nod passing between them - he cannot help but reaffirm that he has he hounded himself so much in the past that he has exhausted his own analysis of what happened to Cath. Doing so had been like sitting on a merry-go-round that didn't stop: you saw the same things over and over again, and then after a while everything became a blur - but it was always the same things, the same blur. Sitting on Parliament Hill again, conscious of a potential new instalment in his life hanging in the balance, dependant on a spinning coin about to land, he cannot help but once again throw himself back onto the ride, hoping for a different outcome yet fearing it will be as it always has been.

Perhaps the one person who can really help him is Beth; perhaps she has helped him already. He wonders if it is possible that another reason for his nervousness - in addition to his need to work out what happens next, which is why he is here in the first place - is an inkling that *she* may hold the key, possess the ability to decipher it all for him, to unravel the past, to cast it in a new light. Is he afraid that there is so much more at stake than he first thought, not just mapping out his future but the rewriting of history; the history he has moulded, shaped and, at some profound level, learned to inhabit - even if there are elements of it which are far from comfortable? Perhaps Beth has the key to turn the merry-go-round off.

At the time all Rico did was to continue following his own agenda, which ultimately made the merry-go-round spin even faster. Indeed, in one sense he may even have been the one responsible for starting it up in the first place.

The next Neil heard from him was a brief note a couple of weeks later in the envelope containing his cheque. The latter had appeared sufficiently impressive for Neil to want to show it to Cath.

"That's a bit more like it," she had said. "Will there be any more where that came from? Is your friend Rico going to put more work your way? After all, we could do with getting our hands on as much money as possible; for the future, I mean."

Although her motivation was patently different to his and totally aligned to the achievement of the longer-term goals she assumed were shared, Neil has subsequently wondered whether that sliver of encouragement from her - of endorsement, even - allowed Rico to push the door open wide. Or for Neil to pull it open for him. His interpretation was that Cath had effectively provided him with an excuse to take *any* work; an excuse which could be argued to be entirely supportive of *her* plan, even if Neil's heart wasn't in it. He now chooses to believe (though for how long he has done so he cannot say) that the most significant part of him would have eventually come round, and - as with the wedding - he would fall into line. It is, perhaps, mitigation of a dishonest sort; a salve based on the knowledge that, even though he had been determined not to cave in, the Neil back then had been a fundamentally weak individual, a weakness that surely would have made capitulation inevitable. And what about now? How resolute is this present incarnation of himself?

When Rico's next offer came it was delivered without frills.

"I have a small interest in a publishing company," he began, the two of them sitting in a Starbucks' just off Shaftesbury Avenue, "one that produces a couple of monthly titles. Gentlemen's magazines."

The pause before his last two words had been far less pronounced that the eyebrow Neil had raised in response. Rico had smooched out a laugh.

"Not quite, Neil," he said, as if rebutting an accusation. "Top shelf they may be - unfairly in my view - but they are nothing like 'Knave' or 'Playboy'. There are articles on lifestyle, fashion, trends."

"And scantily clad young women," Neil suggested.

Rico named the titles.

"If you know them... Well, you'll know the women are hardly clad at all!" It was an invitation to laugh.

Neil picked up his coffee with an 'I'm listening' gesture.

"You won't be surprised to know that Amanda and Claire have appeared in them on occasion. For adverts or clothes promotions mainly."

"But not entirely."

Rico inclined his head slightly.

"Indeed."

"Which explains why they were so 'professional'." Neil recalled their earlier conversation.

Rico smiled.

"I must confess to a little subterfuge on my part. When you were doing the calendar, I asked them to let me know if they thought you would be up to a shoot for one of the magazines."

"And what did they say?"

"To be frank," Rico picked up his own cup, suddenly more serious, "at the end of the first day the reports were not in the least encouraging. I was surprised, frankly."

"And after the second day?"

Rico allowed himself a sip of coffee before responding.

"Entirely different - as you might imagine. And, of course, the end result speaks for itself."

There was a brief hiatus as Neil endeavoured to decipher what Rico had said, convinced more than ever that the truth lay just beneath - rather than on - the surface.

"If it helps, you could think of it as portraiture of sorts. In spite of what people may think or the impression given, the skill, the art, is all in capturing the girls' faces. The rest is…"

"Window dressing?"

Rico laughed at the notion.

"There's a shoot I need completing in the next couple of weeks for one of the up-coming editions. I have someone who could do it for me - I've used him more than once - but I'd quite like you to have a go. Slightly more luxurious surroundings than that loft you've already used. More soft furnishings... And I can get Ray to do the lighting, if you like working with him."

"Is it Claire or Amanda?"

Rico shook his head.

"No; someone else. Someone equally 'professional'. You won't be disappointed."

The suggestion hung between them. Rico pulled a pen from his pocket and scribbled on Neil's unused napkin. A pound-sign followed by some numbers.

"Would that work?"

✿

Sex had never been a problem for Neil. At least he had never considered it as such. Prompted by his memory of the conversation with Rico - and that proposition of his! - the sight of two attractive young women walking past him arm-in-arm continues to trap him in re-evaluation, further consideration of how he had been back then. The ground beneath him was to shift quickly - how could it not? - but at that precise moment, when Rico said "would that work?", he could only have regarded himself as a normal man with normal desires.

His first sexual fumblings prior to university had been inadequate and disappointing, yet they had hinted at future promise. Wasn't that the standard beginning? Varying from the frivolous to the potentially life-changingly serious, his liaisons at college had begun to deliver on that promise. Again, wasn't that normal too, including those few naïve moments when you believed you had uncovered the secret of the universe? He now understood that his experiences back then had been conventional, unsophisticated: mainly boy-on-top, occasionally not; often hurried because of a certain mutual enthusiasm, occasionally not. Haste and panic seemed in the ascendant, rather than revelling in the gift of time bestowed on youth. He was aroused - he assumed - by the same things that aroused most young men. There were acquaintances of both sexes whose reputations suggested a different order, that they had discovered another country from which he was barred; but at the time, none of that had been an issue for him. And later, when Cath approached him on this very hill and said "Do you often take photographs like that?", what that led to was surely just an extension of his sexual journey, built on the lessons he had learned, and the experiences he'd had. And, of course, his love for her.

Qualified by the view through his professional lens, he continues to assume all that 'normal' experience defined his reaction to the girls in the calendar shoot. The fact that Claire and Amanda were attractive had been undermined and devalued by circumstance; even on the second day when their connection with him was on a subtly different level, Neil told himself he had felt only the most vague stirrings for them. Expanding his sexual experience - in any way - had not been something he was looking for, nor something he realised he needed. All of which allowed him to maintain a distance, to keep Cath on the pedestal he had erected for her, and to keep batting away Harry's crude assertion - with a nod and a wink! - of how lucky he was.

And now?

How he had looked at the two young women who had moved past him, how he responded to them - emotionally, rather than sexually - was a product of all the years that followed on from Rico's offer; a journey which today feels as if it had been unavoidable, mapped out for him without his knowledge. He tries reconstruct his image of Claire and Amanda. Although he had little more to do with them, very briefly they were elevated in his estimation to be idealised examples of the female form, only to quickly fall back when superior paragons took their place. Eventually they slipped more or less out of his consciousness, tagged as sad and unfulfilled characters. He knows it had nothing to do with them per se, and everything to do with him. He was the one on the journey. During the two years following Rico's question, it was as if his car were going faster and faster; through the window everything looked different even though in reality it wasn't. You saw different things - missed different things - you made assumptions, filled-in gaps, mistook one thing for another; and the faster the car went, the more distorted the world became. Just like the carousel. Rico had provided the vehicle, and the calendar had seen him slip it into second gear; "would that work?" changed it up into third - and there were still two more gears to go.

And if Beth were to be standing before him now, as she will be in less than twenty minutes? How does this history and experience, his knowledge of himself, of sex, of *that* relationship - how does all that reflect on how he feels about her?

Neil smiles. The question is irrelevant. He is a different person now.

✿

"It doesn't pay to use real names. Compromises the future."

She introduced herself as Sophie, breezing into the flat late enough for Neil and Ray to already be on their second cups of coffee. They had both arrived promptly and while Ray, already familiar with the layout of the place, started setting-up his lighting rigs, Neil wandered through the three main rooms trying to frame shots in his mind and calm his nerves. Two of the rooms were furnished as bedrooms - which is to say they both contained a bed and little else. The divans were luxuriously dressed and on the peripheries there were bold pictures on the walls, expensive-looking curtains on the windows. In terms of composition, there was little imagination required, and Neil's agitation - along with the feeling he had made a mistake - grew. In the lounge two large sofas dominated, with a variety of rugs on the floors. It was a flat no-one could live in. The large lounge windows opened out onto a small balcony which overlooked the river and, from fourteen floors up, offered spectacular views. He was in the process of retrieving his camera to capture the skyline when the front door opened and Sophie walked in.

"Hi Ray," she said, seeing the other man emerging from one of the bedrooms. It was at that point, having just released Neil's hand, she made the comment about not using real names, then immediately excused herself and headed for the bathroom, a travel bag slung over her shoulder. "I'll get ready," she said.

Neil had been unimpressed. He glanced at Ray to try and gauge a reaction but there was none, the latter simply disappearing back into the bedroom from which he had emerged. Unsure what he had expected, the only thing of which Neil was certain was that Sophie wasn't it. Consciously or not, he had established Claire and Amanda as yardsticks of a sort, and based on that brief first impression - the plainness that extended from her face through to the somewhat drab and ordinary clothes she was wearing - Sophie didn't come up to scratch. Yes, she was a little taller, but other than that there was nothing about her which transcended the ordinary. The gnawing sensation of a mistake having been made intensified. Alone in the lounge once more, he completed the action that had been interrupted, fitting a wide-angle lens to his Canon and taking it out onto the balcony. Somewhere in the distance, merged into the horizon, was Parliament Hill, and there someone was almost certainly looking down on him. He tried to click his thoughts away.

"Shall we make a start?"

He had been focused on a barge making its slow way east against the running tide when she spoke. He turned. Although she had merely applied make-up and was now standing with a dressing gown draped about her, it was as if a different person had emerged from the bathroom. Not applied in a heavy-handed way, the cosmetics had transformed her face, elevating her eyes, her cheeks, her lips from out of the ordinary. Especially her lips. It was a transformation that applied to her hair too; now brushed out, it was full, luxuriant. Neil could not help but take her all in, from the crown of her head to the slim black stilettos she was wearing.

She laughed softly at his reaction.

"Is that better?" she asked playfully. Perhaps such a response as his was not unique. "I suppose Rico hasn't given you any instructions or told you what he wants?"

Neil walked a step back into the room, the river and the barge forgotten.

"Nothing specific. He told me to use my imagination."

She laughed again.

"*My* imagination, more like!" There was a short pause. "You've not done this kind of thing before, have you? I mean, I know about the calendar; Mandy told me about that. But that's all, right?"

He nodded, conscious that the room felt suddenly warmer - and that Ray had entered it. For a split second he wondered if the two were linked, something to do with the lighting.

"Well" she said, moving towards him and placing a hand on his arm, "the first thing we need to do is to get you comfortable." She smiled and walked to the balcony. "Such a great view from here," she said, and then slipped the dressing gown from her shoulders and stood naked against the railing looking out onto the city. From over her shoulder she said "Well? How about a few shots just to get warmed up?"

Momentarily frozen as if she had cast a spell on him, Neil could think of nothing, his brain entirely occupied with processing what his eyes were seeing. Sophie's legs seemed impossibly long and slender, joined to her torso at exquisitely shaped hips, the profile of her pelvic bone visible through the rise of her skin. In profile, her breasts, whilst not large, seemed perfectly formed, and Neil had a sudden vision of Harry who would undoubtedly refer to them as being 'like ski jumps' - for him the pinnacle of such compliments.

"Will I do?" she teased, and when he did not immediately reply said provocatively "Well, are you going to use that thing or just cradle it in your hands?"

Neil moved to the sofa where he had placed his camera bag and replaced the wide-angle lens with something more mid-range. He had promised himself a second DSLR to avoid such faffing; perhaps the time had come. When he stood back up and turned again to the window, Sophie was already in character, gradually arching and moving her body as if she were showing it off, not merely to him but to the entire city. Neil lifted the camera to his eye, hardly able to comprehend what he was seeing through the viewfinder.

He pressed the shutter release.

✻

In the end he kept only one photograph from that entire shoot.

However inappropriate, he remembers the events of that morning with wry amusement, not at the events themselves but in the knowledge that people walking past him now - an inconspicuous man in his very late thirties sitting on a Parliament Hill bench - could have no clue as to what he had once done not very many miles from here. There was a chance that someone might recognise him (for other reasons, of course) but it was a possibility so remote that it flashed through his mind and was gone. "Aren't you....?"

He had spent the next couple of days selecting and refining the shots he had taken. Rico had asked for twenty-five to choose from. Getting from the near three-hundred he had taken down to a long-list of fifty had been easy enough, but the final short-list? For the best part of two days he had been glued to his computer monitor, turned from voyeur to artisan (or was it the other way around?) trying to distance himself from Sophie and the emotions of the day in order to concentrate on composition, lighting, sharpness, cropping, tints, special effects. Cath had made nothing more than perfunctory enquiries about the shoot; the fact that she was out all day gave him the freedom to work without having to keep looking over his shoulder. In a gesture he never really understood, he emailed Harry one of the long-list photos that never made it to the final cut. Harry's response was an email simply filled with exclamation marks.

Some six years after, as part of the purge through which he forced himself - that period of self-remodelling - he deleted all traces of the photographs except one, which he would later have printed 24x18 in black-and-white, framed, and hung on the wall of his studio. In it, Sophie is leaning on the balcony facing the river. At that precise moment she had her head turned slightly to one side in order to watch something in the distance, a movement which caused a certain tension in her calves, thighs, lower back. Neil, having been kneeling on the floor at this point - already using *his* imagination! - was looking slightly up at her, the camera perfectly capturing the exquisite contours of her thighs and buttocks, the hint of her genitalia, and framed between her slightly spread legs, the skyline, the other side of the river, London. In the final edit he had cropped the image to just above her shoulders and tightly at the sides to where her hands rested on the balcony. Anonymous in its own way, Neil likes to think he did so out of respect for Sophie - that desire of hers not to use real names! He has always believed it is a good photograph, and it is his alone. He never included it in the twenty-five he sent to Rico.

Of course the significance was never really in that photo; nor, indeed, the entire shoot. It had moved him along professionally - albeit down a path he had not foreseen and would never have proactively chosen - and the end result, a little like the calendar before it, demonstrated he had something of a 'knack'. Rico, delighted once again, had, when the opportunity first presented itself, immediately taken him back to their initial conversation.

"Trust," he had said. "Just like I told you. In fact, I don't think I've ever seen Sophie looking quite like that with anyone else."

Although he had not elaborated, nor described exactly what he meant, Neil had an inkling even then. It was an inkling that was to burgeon into knowledge over time, bolstered, supported and proven with similar experiences - many that went beyond that day with Sophie. He is cognisant of what subsequent events said about *him*, his only comfort being that, as he sits here now - that invisible thirty-something - he has learned to accept the past and his role in it.

Ultimately, if it was never about the photographs, then it wasn't really about Sophie either. Although she had been 'professional' during the first part of the shoot, it was only toward the end, after a short bathroom break, that she really came into her own. The final session in the second bedroom with her releasing all inhibitions, was breathtaking. The fact that she had emerged from the bathroom for those last photographs more relaxed, more uninhibited, Neil had ascribed to her simply doing her job. It was only much later - and after more than one other such episode with other models - that Neil realised she had taken the opportunity to indulge in what might be termed 'a loosener'. Years on, Neil is reconciled to all of that too: to the models, their modus operandi. He has also squared away that particular session, the journey it started him on - even though what it truly meant was only to become clear a little later. What Sophie did that morning - her pose on the balcony, the way she positioned herself on the bed, some of the encouragement she gave him to "get closer", to "make me want you" - was not just to develop him as a photographer, but to change him as a man.

By the end of the session he no longer wanted to photograph her, he wanted desperately to fuck her, and in a way he had never wanted anyone before.

Neil knows he tried to keep that frustration hidden from himself for a while. Even now - separated from it by time and the warm afternoon sun, caressed by the sound of people talking, children playing, the thrum of the city - it still haunts him as a charge from which no amount of self-defence can provide absolution. If memories come with emotions attached so that when they are recalled there should be a natural response - a smile, a frown, a wistful shake of the head - what was the bequest of that morning's session with Sophie other raw desire? Perhaps even now it is still far too complex to categorise and catalogue, not because of what it was, in and of itself, because of what it came to represent.

He re-explores the nooks and crannies of his life as an essential prerequisite, to remind himself of all those things he needs to take into consideration before Beth arrives because they *all* have some influence over what happens next. Doing so, he sees himself back at the same flat again two weeks later, walking into the living room to find Ray already preparing to leave.

"Everything's set-up," he had said, "I just need to show you what to switch on and off, and when." His confusion must have been obvious. "Dee's a slightly more private character than Sophie," Ray explained, "which seems a contradiction in terms, considering... But there you are. She doesn't mind being photographed, but she doesn't like being watched."

Neil recalls trying to square that particular circle as he followed Ray from room to room, assimilating instructions, deciding as soon as Ray had left that he would switch everything on immediately and then everything off at the end of the shoot, just to keep it simple.

The photographs he took of Dee eventually went the same way as those of Sophie, expunged from his life a few years later. This time he didn't keep any at all. What was the point once he had graduated to trophy-hunting?

He had been surprised by her nervousness. It is the first thing he recalls about her, and that always makes him smile. She had arrived in a blaze of colour: bright red coat, vivid skin-tight blue jeans, multi-coloured scarf to match. Naturally pretty, she was shorter than Sophie, and when she eventually undressed, more compact, more athletic. There had been no joking about imagination this time, and he remembers how he had decided to adopt the same approach as before, starting with a few relaxed shots in the lounge. Dee, showing no interest in the balcony, appeared instantly serious, as if she were concentrating in a way Sophie hadn't. It wasn't as if she was concerned or protecting herself, but rather working at what she should be doing, how she should look, how she should *be*. There was effort and calculation involved; that the role she had to play did not seem to come to her naturally suggested a different kind of past, one with a history. And perhaps she was weighing him up, too.

During the session in the first bedroom - freshly dressed with different bedding, pictures and drapes - she seemed slightly more at ease. Neil recalls moments of levity, some banter; he remembers that the more he looked through his lens, the more he saw of her. She had a small mole at the top of her right thigh, a tiny birthmark at the base of her spine. Had he felt the first stirrings then? He must have.

When they got into the second bedroom it was roasting; the effect of having Ray's lights on for so long. He remembers asking her if he could open the window, and then the next thing she was there beside him, lifting his t-shirt over his head, taking his free hand and placing it on her right breast.

Neil looks around, conscious that he may be blushing, concerned that his memories might somehow be leaking out to create a hologram visible to his fellow park patrons. If so, they show no sign of having spotted it. A couple walking their black spaniel, lively and agitated as all spaniels need to be, stroll by obliviously; a boy and girl, engaged in a foot race which the boy will win, flash by without pause. Satisfied but not exactly contented, he is compelled to return to the scene, the frantic almost animalistic coupling, and when he came, the release feeling like nothing he had ever experienced before. He had laid next to her until she had said "Shall we take the last shots now? Just give me five minutes.". While she was in the bathroom, he hurriedly dressed, tried to compose himself by fiddling with his camera, walking into the lounge and the first bedroom to turn off the lights. He tried not to think.

Even if he did not know it at the time, he soon realised that those final photographs had a different quality about them. Inevitably they possessed an intimacy he had never managed to achieve in anything he had previously taken. He remembers explicitly thinking of Cath and not Dee the first time he came to the editing process. It wasn't about what he had done - and what he should *not* have done - nor about what it meant or said, or where it might lead; he was thinking only about the photographs and the quality they possessed. There was something new and authentic and genuine about them. Even though they were, he knew, soft porn, those final shots of Dee were, above all, *honest*.

Inevitably Rico loved them - and this time Harry remained ungifted.

As he shifts his position slightly on the bench, crossing his legs at the ankle rather than the knee, he frowns.

❋

"Can I take your photo?"

Cath turned her head from the pillow to look at him.

"What a funny thing to ask." She was evidently amused. "Of course you can; you've always been able to."

Neil rolled away from her and swung his feet to the floor.

"Now?"

The word hit him square in the back, and in the move of the mattress he sensed her prop herself up a little. They had just made love for the first time in a little while, a slow and gentle process that had unwrapped itself like the petals of a flower caught in slow time-lapse. Yet he had wanted it to be different. He had wanted something more aggressive, animal; brutal almost. Ever since his experience with Dee, he had been constructing scenarios in his head where those raw feelings of lust and desire had been transferred to Cath, overlaid and enriched by the love he felt for her; he had imagined the coming together of such sensations would, in some way, deliver the most he could ever hope for from sex. But Cath had never been that way inclined; she was all subtlety, gentleness and patience in their love-making. He wondered if that played to some ideal *she* had. Whatever their separate motivations, whenever they'd had intercourse and experienced each other intimately it had been constrained by her approach. Based on the final photographs he had taken of Dee, Neil assumed any he took of Cath now would be equally honest and authentic, and portray her in the most genuine way possible.

He glanced over his shoulder to where she had pulled the duvet up across her chest. Undeniably, it was an protective gesture.

"Just for me," he said limply, knowing he had already been denied.

"I don't think so," she said, the softest tones gone from her voice. "Not for you or anyone."

Turning away from her, he looked down into his lap, his flaccid penis, his thighs, the rucked-up bedding. For a moment he felt paralysed, uncertain as to what his next move should be.

"So how have you found it?"

He and Rico were back in the Soho Starbuck's the following day. It had become their regular haunt for what Rico liked to call their 'business meetings'.

"In what sense?" Neil asked.

"Photographically, of course. Professionally."

It was a word that now hung strangely between them, layered with meanings it hadn't possessed when they first met. Neil found himself wondering if Dee had said anything to him.

"You've seen the output," Neil said, as if his photographs were an extension of him, proof of something, the answer to any question anyone might ever ask.

"Indeed; and I couldn't be happier. I won't mention the 'T-word' again, I promise, but it's clear you have it in spades. Dee doesn't open herself up to just anyone."

Momentarily wondering how innocent that last phrase had been, Neil then dismissed it and looked around the café. With its standard decor, standard layout, they could have been almost anywhere in the world; and yet there was something about the place that suggested Soho, that Shaftesbury Avenue was nearby, and not far from there the less salubrious side of London. He tried to trace the line between how he had started, that first

Condé Nast show, and here; it had a trajectory he suddenly didn't want to think about.

"There's an opportunity here for a regular stream of work." Rico had carried on speaking. "Guaranteed income, if you will. I'm not naïve enough to argue that it's Fine Art, but it would take the pressure off financially, and give you time to devote to your other more important projects. And you can do with with your eyes closed - though obviously you can't!" Rico laughed at his own joke. "It won't always be at the flat either; there are one or two other locations we use, some out of town." He paused. "What do you think?"

Neil drained his remaining quarter cup of coffee in one go.

"When's the next one?"

❊

It might have been about to rain judging by the look on Neil's face as he sits on the bench, his frown seeming to forecast a downpour of biblical proportions. Yet the sky remains almost cloudless, and it is still warm. The darkness he succumbed to in that moment was a purely local one, bleeding out from the memory of what happened next. He knows he could shake himself out of it, get up to walk it off, preoccupy himself with his phone and the backstop of its multi-megapixel camera - but he does none of those things. Having begun a process, he needs to conclude it; the last thing he can do is face Beth having bailed out half way through. Taking the easy route - although attractive in the short-term - always comes back to bite you. Doesn't he know that to his cost?

After the Soho meeting with Rico, things happened quickly - not that he was aware of it at the time. He looks back on himself as being absurdly comfortable in the silent eye of the storm as it began to rage about him.

One commission followed another. Rico was as good as his word; always a different girl, a variety of locations. The outcome in terms of the photographs were of an acceptable standard, showing the girls off to their absolute best. There was an undeniable quality about them born from intimacy and - yes - trust. And often that intimacy came as a result of more than just the clicking of a shutter, words of encouragement, or instructions on to how to pose, to look. Regularly they came from the last shots of the day, made all the more moody and atmospheric by subdued lighting and the almost inevitable consequence of Ray's departure. He began to get a reputation - and not just as a photographer - yet still the girls still seemed happy to pose for him. Perhaps he represented a challenge to some of them; perhaps they wanted to see what all the fuss was about and were happy to play fast-and-loose. But most of all they just wanted to look good, and within a few months Neil became 'the man' for being able to do that better than anyone else. If he has a regret - and he is still not sure whether 'regret' is entirely the right word - it is that he never saw Sophie again. She felt like unfinished business and he often asked after her, but Rico remained coy, as if she were off-limits.

He recalls turning down a Condé Nast project that previously he would have jumped at. At the time he told himself it was the inadequate money, but he now knows that was not the real reason. Perhaps he knew it then. After he turned down a second, he discovered there would not be an opportunity to reject a third; they simply stopped calling. But one of the major players in Rico's 'genre' *did* call. It had been a policy of their UK editor to monitor the competition, and Neil's shoots had attracted their attention. When they offered him something, he didn't hesitate. He kidded himself he had 'arrived'.

A man is suddenly hovering near him. Wearing slightly too many clothes for the day and the kind of look that says he has lost something, he hesitates. Neil glances at him and away. He wonders if he too has arranged to meet someone there; perhaps it is a new encounter of some kind, and he is wondering if Neil is the person he is supposed to meet. A blind date, of sorts. He braces himself for the approach: "Excuse me, but are you Brian / Colin / Malcolm?". Or perhaps the man has recognised him and is agonising over whether he should introduce himself, say "I saw your exhibition at the Barbican last week" or the more rudimentary "Love your work". Neil recalls how, once he had a dozen of Rico's shoots under his belt, he became paranoid about meeting one of the girls when out with Cath. Would they say hello? Or worse still, would they assume that Cath was like them, another model, another conquest? He recalls how he started to be careful about where they went, where they ate. He nudged them into a narrower but safer set of restaurants and coffee shops, avoided the centre of town as much as possible. He thought he was being shrewd, cautious, clever even.

Although relieved when the man eventually walks away, Neil now displays all the signs of someone in a thunderous mood. He looks around to check that Beth is not nearby; he wouldn't want to see her just yet, not until he has pushed on through the hardest part of all.

✿

It is impossible for him to forget the afternoon Ralph turned up at the flat unannounced.

"I'm worried about Cath," he said once established on the sofa, Neil having made him the obligatory coffee.

"Cath?"

"Please tell me you've noticed, Neil?" Ralph's words were delivered with the air of a man who already knew the answer, proven by the fact that he chose to push on. "She's seems tense, on edge. Like there's something on her mind, something troubling her."

The shame of not having noticed anything didn't hit him until much later, once events had played out. Neil can only remember the degree of surprise he felt, firstly at Ralph's presence, and secondly at the matter at the heart of his concern. He and Cath seemed to have been coasting along without any issues; yes, his work had obviously been taking up a fair amount of his time - and not only time! - but he recalls feeling that he had been pretty successful in keeping all that separate from his private life.

"I know she wants us to start a family, but I'm just not ready yet Ralph." As it seemed he needed to come up with a reason, a source to justify her father's concern, this had been all he could think of. At least it had the advantage of being true. "Perhaps it's that. Perhaps she's frustrated that we haven't agreed to move on yet."

He recalls seeing Ralph struggle with his answer, part of him clearly wanting to accept it, but another part not.

"Yes, I know about that."

Even now, Neil cannot help but be surprised that Ralph was aware of their familial challenges; yet why should he not have been? Cath had been spending a great deal of time at her parents, so when she was there what else were they to talk about? After all this time, he still cannot avoid the regret of not having seen the stresses in her when he needed to.

"But I think there's something else." Ralph had continued as if responding to Neil saying something else. "Could you do me a favour?"

"Of course. Anything."

"Talk to her. Ask her. I'm sure she'll tell you."

"I will."

Perhaps there would never have been a good time for him to broach the subject with her, but because Ralph's visit was fresh in his mind, Neil chose to do so after dinner that same evening - ignoring the fact she said she'd had a tough day at the Museum, and that she was already on her third glass of wine by the time they finished the meal he had prepared: a penne carbonara, something he felt he had off to a tee, and one of Cath's favourites. Seeing her push the pasta around her bowl and leaving half of it unfinished should have been enough of a warning for him to postpone, rather than an argument to push on.

"Your Dad came round this afternoon."

"Daddy?"

Neil nodded, watched her face.

"What did he want?"

"He's worried about you." Neil tried the softest tone he could muster, as if doing so allowed him to be included in her father's concern too.

"Me?"

It was incredulity, not surprise. There was no sign in Cath's expression to indicate she had been found out or had a secret exposed. Neil was prepared to follow-up with what he had said to Ralph, his own appreciation of her frustration. What he was not prepared for was the response she unveiled.

"I'm not the one he should be worried about."

"What's that supposed to mean?"

"I mean, he should be worried about you, not me."

"Me?!" It was an inversion he hadn't seen coming, like driving into a blind bend in the dark and suddenly being faced with full-beam headlights coming straight toward you.

"How's work *really* going, Neil? You tell me that it's good, that you've got new contracts, more money. But why haven't I seen any of the photographs? Why haven't you done anything for Condé Nast for such a long time?"

Neil was suddenly on the defensive.

"Work's good - like I said. Yes, there's more of it, and more money too. Nothing to worry about there, if that's what's bothering you." He waited for a response and the glimmer of a way out from what felt like a trap into which he had unwittingly stumbled. None came. "Why haven't you seen any of the photos? I don't know. Maybe because you haven't seemed that interested in what I've been doing for some time. And anyway, fashion and that sort of thing doesn't really float your boat, does it?"

"'Fashion': is that what they call it now?"

"Call what?"

Cath drained her glass, poured the last of the wine into it, then stood to take the empty bottle through to the kitchen.

"I'm not stupid, Neil. I have friends, friends with husbands, husbands with eyes. You might at least have had the common sense - the decency - to use a false name. I need you to think about what you're doing and why you're doing it. I need you to decide what's important, because I don't want to become any more of a laughing stock than I currently am. I want the future that we talked about; the one *I* want. And I need to know that's what you want too. Is what you're doing *really* how you wanted your career to develop? I thought you had greater aspirations than that; I thought you were serious."

He reached out a hand as she passed him, but she edged far enough away to remain out of reach.

❖

As it stretches between him and the horizon, the city seems both impersonal and impervious. Uncaring. It is something he is used to, comfortable with. It hadn't been the same back then when his attachment to it had been supremely naïve. Perhaps it is only natural for youth to assume it enjoys a symbiotic relationship with London especially when, in his case, the theory was supported by his experiences with Rico, the girls, places where they held the shoots. Especially the girls. His intoxication - because he now knows that's what it was - existed on many levels, the city being their broker. However, it was an addiction to be shattered soon enough, after which came the Cold Turkey, the agony, the realisation. That relationship - the fabled, mythological one he thought he enjoyed - is something after which he no longer hankers; rather, he now feels as if London tolerates him as much as he tolerates it. Perhaps there is a grudging respect - in equal measure to suspicion and distrust. The journey from where he was that evening with Cath to where he is now, sitting on a park bench overseeing a kingdom more as archaeologist than anything else, was at times a brutal one.

If he had to mark the moment when Cath's relationship with him changed irreparably, Neil always comes back to that evening - even if secretly he knows it fractured much earlier. He still wonders if it is coincidental that he never made carbonara for her again.

The following day she seemed more like her old self, almost as if the conversation the previous evening had been something he had dreamed. But it had seen the planting of a seed that was to instantly germinate - and which Neil was to continue to water. As it grew, the roots of change spread beneath the surface, quickly, almost imperceptibly: minor modifications to their routine; Cath spending more time at work or at her parents; fewer moments of intimacy; shallower conversations. As he became gradually untethered from her, Neil found a need to be anchored elsewhere, and the only option open to him was his work - which meant Rico and the girls. Consequently, if Cath had hoped that her intervention would make him think twice about his current career path, it only succeeded in promoting the exact opposite: he took on more work - long since having given up the dregs of his old 'day job' - and increasingly sought solace with his models whenever the opportunity arose. The circle was both vicious and downward.

Although he did so unobtrusively, Rico took full advantage of Neil's relative instability, offering him an increasing range of opportunities, some more socially mainstream, most not. Becoming indiscriminate in the work he accepted is not something upon which he can look back with any pride, but he was addicted - to the work and to the release and comfort some of the models (driven by their own agendas, no doubt) seemed only too willing to provide. The whole cocktail offered him a buffer, an emotional neutral zone between himself and Cath. He only realised it later, but she stopped talking about a house and family.

"I'm sorry, Old Fruit, but I think you're on the verge of having to make up your mind."

He and Harry had been sitting in a bar not far from Leicester Square, the city's pre-Christmas lights beginning to emerge in shop windows and around lamp posts. It was the time of year where the cold and the dark made you look forward to the festivities - and fear the two months that followed them. Ralph's visit was four months behind him.

"In what way?"

"Well, from what you've told me you've clearly been rumbled. That quote about friends and husbands and eyes; Cath knows the kind of photographs you've been taking, what your work consists of."

"Why should it matter? I mean, it's just work."

"Just?"

"I go out, take photos, come home" - Neil ducked the question - "then I work on the shots - edit, crop, enhance - and someone pays me for my trouble. Pays me well enough. Most of the money I earn goes on the flat, our living, some into savings. Isn't that okay? Doesn't that get us closer to what she wants?"

"Does it?" Harry let the question hang unanswered just long enough for it to register. "How would you feel if Cath were one of the models? If she went out of a morning, peeled off her kit for some guy to take photos of her, and then justified it in the same way you just have; 'it's just work, money'?"

Ironically, perspective - in life, at least - wasn't one of Neil's strong suits; not then, in any event. He hopes he has learned enough to now have a more rounded view. Not having examined the situation from any angle other than his own, he recalls Harry's hypothesis striking home. As did his follow-up.

"Your problem, my friend, is one of bread. You want it buttered on both sides. Which is all well and good, but sooner or later you're going to drop it - that's inevitable - and one side or the other is going to get dirty and become inedible. I think you need to decide which side of the bread you want to keep clean. And quick. Because I think it's on it's way to the floor as we speak."

And it was, slipping from his grasp as he attempted to retrieve it, eventually leaving both sides spoiled.

✻

"How would you feel if I told you I was having a baby?"

Had that been her last card, the final throw of the dice? She had delivered it out of a silence broken only by the inane chatter from a TV gameshow, their evenings together having descended into an uninspiring pit of routine.

Neil looked across to where she sat, her eyes resolutely fixed on the television, features set, giving nothing away. It was only when she was certain he was looking at her that she turned her head his way.

"Well?"

His mind raced through the options, not only of what to say out loud, but what not to say; of the two, he had no problem populating the second list. He found himself asking questions of his own, like 'how is that possible?' and 'when is it due?' - and remains ashamed to this day to recall the fleeting 'who's the father?'. In the end, there was no safe haven. She had placed a landmine in front of him and he had stepped on it before he knew what was happening.

"Are you?" was all he could muster.

"I didn't say I was; but I want to know how you would feel if I were. If *we* were."

"But you're not?"

"I didn't say I wasn't either." Her exasperation manifested itself as a blend of smile and grimace, impossible for Neil to read. She tried for the third time. "I just want to know how you would feel about it, either way."

Knowing he could muster no answer acceptable to her, he felt the trap close.

"I don't know. I'd be a bit stunned, I suppose, not having planned it. And then we'd need to think about what it meant for the future," he glanced briefly around the room, trying to decide if the flat were somehow complicit in all of this, and whose side it was on, "you know, this place, your work - all that stuff."

Letting the dust settle a little, the room still reverberating from the explosion she had initiated, Cath looked back at the television. A couple were trying to decide whether to stick with the money they had won thus far or to gamble it all on one final question.

"And that's your answer?" She addressed her words as much to the gameshow as to him; so much so, that Neil was forced to check whether she might be berating the contestants for making a wrong choice.

But her statement was aimed solely at him.

"Well I'm not," she said, still not looking his way. "Which is probably just as well, wouldn't you say?"

That one was much easier for Neil to answer, but he kept his counsel, a burst of applause from the television seeming an adequate enough response.

✽

Below him, the city talks to its inhabitants. Everywhere there are lights and muffled sounds, beeps and bangs and crashes all striving to convey their own message: 'stop', 'go', 'buy', 'enjoy'. Like everyone else, these are signs he takes for granted because they are ever-present, chattering and flashing, a soundtrack that goes with the territory; if one becomes blind to them, you do so out of complacency more than anything else. His ignoring of the signs Cath sent him during those months after Ralph's visit - including the bizarre baby-talk - was not induced by habit but arrived at out of choice. Six years on that is all too clear; painful self-knowledge he has lived with for some time.

Later - during that time when he felt he had needed to protect himself - he argued that she had not been explicit enough, had been far too subtle for him. Selfishly, it had been an attempt to shift the blame. "I didn't know; she didn't say" was his mantra for a short while. And yet he *had* known, unconsciously at least; and later still he found himself able to promote fragments of memory into the spotlight from the negatives of their life together. It became a litany, a quest of sorts; once he had embraced his failure, he went out of his way to seek examples and incidents through which he could chastise himself: specific conversations; things said or not said; an unguarded look; a complaint. And then, very occasionally, the explicit - like the day she almost begged him to stop working for Rico. He recalls things he said, promised he made, commitments to change. At the time he excused all those away too.

Had that dredging through the evidence of his abject failure been the low point? It was difficult to say. When he fell into the trough his first reaction was that somehow *he* was the victim, that blame lay elsewhere: with Rico, the city, Harry, even Cath herself. Eventually looking hard into the mirror, perhaps seeing the truth of things plunged him into the real darkness.

He had been working particularly hard. Rico had lined up three back-to-back shoots, all deadline-driven, one a highly lucrative deal of limited cultural value with a 'red top' newspaper. In consequence he had been out of the house early most days that last week; out early and back late, and then working into the small hours editing the photographs. And he hadn't just been working with his camera, either. As he became more tired - and more divorced from his 'normal' life - he pushed the girls harder, both in terms of what they would do for the camera and what they would do for him. He has ceased to pretend he doesn't recognise the person he was then; no longer claims he was too punch-drunk, like a boxer on the ropes. If he has previously told himself that he can't remember the names of the girls who, one way or another, offered him solace, then he was lying about that too.

It had been after eight when he got back to the flat on the Thursday evening. There had been a shoot in the riverside flat during the morning and into the afternoon. The model - Cindy, one of Neil's favourites - had stayed behind after Ray left. Later, he had gone into town for a pre-arranged drink with Rico only to be let down at the last minute, his client claiming urgent business. Unable to get hold of Harry too, he had found himself eating alone at a basement Pizza Express listening to a set of somewhat monotone jazz of dubious quality. He has never been able to explain - to himself or anyone else - why he hadn't simply gone home.

He found Cath lying on the bed. On the bedside table, a bottle of wine stood a quarter full and a small plastic bottle one-hundred percent empty.

His attempts to rouse her - frantic and panic-stricken, accompanied by shouts and tears - proved ineffective, and within seconds he had phoned 999. All he could do was to cradle her limp body in his arms as he waited for the tell-tale sound of the ambulance, the city giving out another sign. He remembers wondering if he should call Ralph, deciding to wait until he knew what was going on, until Cath had been seen, assessed, revived. That had been selfish too, his desire to be able to paint a more rosy picture for her father.

When they arrived, the paramedics had been fast and efficient, easing him away to allow them to do their job. It was as if he had become suddenly superfluous - though he was to gradually recognise he had been increasingly peripheral for Cath for some time. They intubated her, gave her an injection, strapped her to a trolley. Only when they were wheeling her to the ambulance did they seem to remember he was there; the invitation to accompany the three of them to the hospital felt like an afterthought.

As he has done sporadically for the last half-hour or so, Neil attempts to secure the location of those final scenes in the sprawl below him. St Mary's, Paddington. What does he remember of it now? That the panic never left him, not in the ambulance nor in the hospital; that he had talked at her constantly throughout the short blue-lit journey; that he had begged and cried. And that he had hated himself.

The hospital conformed as it had to: hot, stark, filled with the bustle of staff in uniforms, porters with trolleys, patients shuffling along dragging saline drip stands behind them, some heading for outside air and the blessed release of a cigarette. They left him in a corridor staring at an anonymous blue door beyond which people attended to his wife. When people came and went, quickly and urgently, in and out of the room, they all avoided his eye, said nothing. On the walls of the corridor hung numerous large photographs of various members of staff, all smiling, captured in black-and-white, and beside each a small card with their name, their role. They were comforting; images of people who conveyed a common message: "it will be all right".

Except it wasn't.

Three

And neither was the following day the hardest. Irrespective of what he believed or how he felt, the organisational juggernaut personified by Ralph kicked into gear and Neil was relegated to a role of taking phone calls and answering questions. Which was just as well. If he is honest with himself he knows that Friday he felt nothing. Or perhaps it is more accurate to say that he didn't really know what to feel; he was in a vacuum for twenty-four hours. He can claim to have experienced everything expected of him - loss, pain, anguish, anger - but in what dosage he was (and remains) unable to articulate. Collectively and individually they seemed peripheral emotions, as if they were being experienced by someone else, or as if he had been able to abstract himself from them. He remembers a brief phone call with Harry which had been painful; and one with Rico which had been less so. Neil cried-off work commitments for the following week, a period which eventually extended to nearly three.

The city left him alone too. Looking at it now, pulsing beneath him, he still struggles to understand how the fabrications we overlay upon time can make so much of a difference. There is nothing truly unique one day to the next; the risings of the sun and moon are the results of disinterested natural programming, and he feels it is only when we impose an artificial structure upon them - the notions of 'the working day' or 'the working week' - people get into difficulty. And that is what Saturday gifted him, a low blow, enough to wind him and double him up. It was a non-working day, a lay-in day, a day for pottering, shopping, walking, eating; it was a day when - whatever the recent state of their marriage might have been - he did all those things with Cath. So when he woke in a half-empty bed, rose to make just a single cup of coffee, a half-portion of breakfast, to sit numbed on the sofa watching early-morning television chat shows for something to do, only then did he start to have an inkling of the depth of the chasm into which he had fallen.

Towards the end of the morning he tried to rouse himself to action, to do something. He settled on losing himself in town, and the notion of wandering the National Gallery - partly to subsume himself in a crowd and partly as an act of homage - came to him suddenly and decisively. In less than fifteen minutes he was out of the flat and walking to the tube station where, on arrival, he found a sign saying there were disruptions and delays on all lines due to a fire in a tunnel near Waterloo. Unable to face the prospect of standing around on a crowded platform, he immediately gave up. Taking the bus would have been an option, but already uncertain as to how he would react to the expedition, he had sold himself the idea of the underground because it was faster, easier for him to bail out at any point, turn around, and get home quickly should the need arise. On the way back from the station he stopped in the local 'one-stop shop' and bought milk and bread, some fresh croissants, a newspaper - not because he needed any of those things, but because it seemed the right thing to do.

Later, cocooned on the sofa with tea and the remnants of lunch, his watching televised live sport he wasn't interested in was interrupted by Cynthia, Cath's mother; a rare excursion for her. She had come, she said, to see if he was okay, if there was anything he needed, and to give herself another chance to cry. Once that was out of the way, she confessed to having some questions from Ralph where Neil's input was needed. It was only later, after the funeral, that he realised Ralph had been too angry to come and ask them himself. Should he have been surprised? Does he remain surprised even now? Ralph clearly felt that Neil had betrayed his daughter and in doing so betrayed him. He had trusted him with his daughter's life and Neil had failed the test; from a father's perspective it was as simple as that.

He allows his eyes to scan the city once more, this time in an unfocussed way, deliberately skipping the general location of the church where they had held the funeral, a ceremony totally opposite to their wedding in terms of scale, grandeur and pomp. Whether or not it had been appropriate, he had never questioned Ralph's motivation for such a low-key send-off. Clearly it was no celebration; there was no glorying in an untimely end, simply because the end was not fitting at all. Ever since that dark day, Neil has come to rationalise that his presence had only ever been endured by Ralph under sufferance - something magnified a thousand-fold with his belief that Neil had been the catalyst for Cath's death, that it wasn't suicide at all. Did he feel like a murderer? It was a question that briefly tormented him.

After they parted at the end of that grey and subdued early winter's day - Ralph deliberately managing to avoid a farewell handshake - the two of them never spoke again. There was the odd letter in relation to Cath's effects, and over the next few weeks Cynthia became the physical go-between on those rare occasions when one was needed. Cath had left everything to him in the unmodified wills they had jointly drawn up soon after their marriage, and once those particular and incontrovertible wheels were in motion, Ralph's influence simply ebbed away.

Neil recalls a strange period of limbo, two weeks during which he operated like an automaton, deliberately reducing his existence to the lowest common denominators available. He lived on packet meals and takeaways, and on the infrequent occasions he cooked kept the meals simple. Even though Cynthia had removed all of Cath's clothes and the vast majority of her personal effects, the flat still resonated of her: the occasional surprise in an echo of her perfume, or something found at the back of a drawer. But more than that it was the negative - space and absence - that began to torture him; vacuums were suddenly 'visible' everywhere and evidenced in wardrobes, shelves, cupboards. And he became aware of all the things she had done that he had taken for granted, things he suddenly found were now his responsibility, like cleaning the bathroom and hoovering the carpets. Forced to compile a list of living's mundanities, it was as if he was being re-educated.

"You look fucking dreadful," had been Harry's opening salvo when he came round to see him part-way into his second week of solitary confinement. It was an assessment supported by a small pile of the unwashed - clothes, crockery - and an array of empties Neil hadn't yet taken to the local bottle bank.

"You know how it is," he remembers saying. It had been a ridiculous comment because he knew full-well that Harry *didn't* know how it was. He was learning it for himself, and even now - six years later - is certain there are still pieces of the jigsaw missing.

"When did you last go out?"

"What day is it? It seems I now navigate by the snooker, darts and football on the TV rather than use a conventional calendar."

Harry, who had only just sat down, stood up and, unable to help himself, started to tidy as he spoke.

"What about work? I don't suppose you've done any? Just to take your mind off things."

The notion seemed a strange one, then as much as it does now, Neil recalling their conversation with his mind very much *on* things.

"My cameras haven't been out of their bags since..." It was obvious since when.

"And Rico?"

"Has called a couple of times. Once yesterday in fact. Wants to know when I can do another shoot for him. There's one next week. Says it's low-key, simple, no pressure. Christmas-themed apparently - God help us!"

"So why don't you? Just the one effort before Christmas - though I don't suppose you give a stuff about all that ritual right now... But maybe you should, Old Fruit. Do something relatively normal, I mean. And then maybe go away for a few days over the holiday, somewhere different, just you and your cameras. You can't sit here festering until bloody January otherwise you'll never get out."

Even through the fug that had descended upon him, Neil knew Harry was right.

"That's what Rico said."

"He did?" Harry was unable to keep the surprise from his voice.

"With his own special slant on it, of course."

It had been an attempt at a joke. Which was something.

✧

He had made an effort, showered, put on clean clothes; he had not shaved but rather 'tidied up' the beard he had inadvertently been growing for over two weeks. He knew he could not turn up at the flat looking like a tramp; how he appeared could affect how the model would respond to him. If there was no attraction of any kind, the final images would be flat, antiseptic.

Not only was Ray early as usual - their greeting as perfunctory as ever - but Amanda was there too. It later transpired that, in what could only pass as a gesture of thoughtfulness, Rico assumed it might be easier for Neil to work with someone he already knew. She had kissed him lightly on the cheek when he arrived; they talked about nothing in particular.

It was a morning spent going through the motions, Neil almost relying on muscle-memory to see him through it. He could tell Amanda was trying to pull out all the stops, working hard, exaggerating, taking the odd risk, striving to help him rekindle something. After two hours of the sound of his camera shutter clicking and little else, they began to wrap up. Amanda offered to stay after Ray had left. Neil remembers her offer fondly - and that it felt too much like charity. In any event, he still didn't know what he wanted. Or needed. He declined, and she kissed him again on the cheek when she left, kisses bookending a morning that felt alien, an experiment that hadn't delivered the expected results.

Back at the flat he collapsed in front of the television and made no attempt to review the photographs until the following day. They proved to be derivative, almost amateur; they lacked engagement and passion. Amanda looked stunning, as he knew she would - as she could not help but be - yet the shots gave him the impression of an emotional curtain hanging between the two of them, one which fogged the images. That had to be down to him. Attempting to be as professional as possible, he cropped, tweaked, and selected; then he tweaked again, eventually sending off twenty from which Rico could make his final choice. The email to which they were attached said "Not my best, but hopefully ok. I'm going away for Xmas, so see you in the New Year. Love to Amanda." The comment about going away surprised him with its decisiveness. It was not something he had actively considered let alone settled on doing; perhaps it had been the offspring of Harry's suggestion, lodged in his mind, working its way through to his consciousness without him even realising it.

Rico's email on its way, Neil recalls opening his browser and finding a suitable accommodation booking site on which he selected the relevant filters: dates, type of room, grade of accommodation. He left the location blank, happy to allow chance to play its hand. Considering he was seeking something over Christmas, when the list of available options came back he was surprised just how long it proved to be. He sorted by price, then filtered further, increasing the grade of accommodation and ruling out a range of locations - like the Lake District, Cornwall, Scotland - because they would be too far from London or too busy. It had been something of a random approach given he had no real idea what he was looking for. In the end he settled on Bakewell and a small hotel that seemed just a notch above a B&B. He was drawn to its 'bijou' label, its recent rave reviews, and the promise of home-cooked food.

Looking at the sun glinting off the towers of central London, he recalls the trepidation he felt that morning when, once again, he took the trouble to make himself look as respectable as he could, the mirror presenting back a man suddenly years older than he had previously been. He packed his bag with a surprising degree of nervousness, double-checking its contents as if it were the first time he had done any such thing, the days of Condé Nast relegated to oblivion. Even though the bonds were loosening and in spite of everything - especially a vague sense of betrayal - he still clung to the belief that he and the city were one, leaving it behind amounted to a kind of abandonment. This untying of the knot was verging on the terrifying - amplified by the certain knowledge he would be forced to speak to people he didn't know. Interaction with others loomed before him. And he would be on his own, for the first time in a long while navigating without his Pole Star. More than once as he drove north - joining the M1 at its point of origin and then following it all the way to the south of Chesterfield where he left it to track west - he was tempted by service stations and junctions; the services to delay and dither, the junctions as opportunities to turn around and head back.

Somewhere in the interchange mêlée between the Leicester and Nottingham turnoffs he was assaulted by a confusion as to what 'home' actually meant. It was a word liberally used and rarely understood; at least that was his conclusion. He had taken the flat for granted, as he had his old 'bachelor pad'; it was a place to eat and sleep, to store things. He had never considered it a home. For Cath, had it been little more than a staging post, a stepping stone between her parents' house and what would now be an unfulfilled ambition? In her case, 'home' was to be what came next, what *she* would build - with or without his wholehearted commitment. Seeing that dream recede had surely been a contributing factor to the choices she made, and as such, one of the many black marks against him. Recognising that, Neil also understood he had no competing or comparable notion to hold up against it. What was 'home' for him? Indeed, had the concept ever been relevant? It was not something he'd really considered in any conscious or rational way as a child, and then came university, and after that the first job. He had never regarded the Kentish Town flat as 'romantic' in any way. Even before he met Cath, he knew it would need to be followed by something else - though as to what that might be he'd had no idea. Because of her clear-mindedness, her vision, she had forced upon him a number of 'what happens next?' conundrums - 'home' included - all of which had bred uncertainty in him, in spite of her apparently knowing the answers. But they were now transformed into sores which had started blooming after her death, infected by her absence, fed by the growing number of questions that seemed to now stalk him in plain sight. 'What was home?' was associated with the practical decision he needed to make about the flat: was he going to stay there or move on? And if the latter, where to? Similarly, arriving at a decision about his work and what the future held there was a challenge which had only arisen as a result of his recent experience with Amanda. Not having held his camera for two weeks had already fostered a fading intimacy between he and the tools of his trade; the shoot had not only reacquainted the two of them in a nervous, ham-fisted kind of way, but also posed an associated 'what next?' question there too. Until the morning he walked onto the job he hadn't thought of it at all.

There was a third dilemma too; the one related to his emotional well-being. Home and security, work and financial stability, love. Assailed by this powerful triumvirate of 'what nexts' and feeling himself weakening as he drove, he instinctively knew that going back would not defeat them; returning to the flat and pretending wouldn't make them disappear. If he ran away - in whatever form that might take - and chose not to address those particular foes, he remained sufficiently self-aware to know they would always be there, sitting on his shoulder, constantly nagging, demanding to be satisfied. He entered Bakewell without expectation, not anticipating that the next few days would start tosolve these riddles. But now, five years' of hindsight to the good, he can see how getting away that Christmas had been an essential beginning in recognising there were monsters to be faced down.

✻

There being nothing remarkable about it, the room seemed both alien and comforting at the same time: queen-sized bed, two bedside tables, a chest of drawers, a small wardrobe, one easy chair next to a side table, a television attached to the wall at the foot of the bed. A door to the compact en suite. It was a formula with which he was familiar, yet he was struck by how different it was both from his own bedroom and - even without Ray's lights - the bedrooms in the flat used to fulfil his obligations to Rico. And his own ego. But what struck him most of all was that here was a room he didn't need to think or worry about; it required nothing of him but to be used. Someone else would take care of the sheets, the towels, ensure the tea-making facilities were kept topped-up. In doing so, it was relieving him of the smallest of burdens, absolving him of the thinnest and most superficial layer of worry, as if that were its prime purpose, especially now. He unpacked. In three days - on Boxing Day - he would re-pack then head south.

Unable to help himself, Neil liked his hosts - Abi and Clive - immediately. She was a sharp, precise, middle-aged woman who later would confess to having started out on a high-flying career in the City (Morgan Stanley, EY) before abandoning it in favour of what she liked to call 'a more rudimentary lifestyle'. Clive - also an ex-City man - simply tagged along, and they operated as a traditional front-of-house / back-of-house duet. Or at least that's what the guests saw during their public moments. It was a natural division of labour given Clive had only started working in the City once a career as a chef failed to take-off, something - Abi whispered, in confidence! - more down to lack of drive than lack of talent. Their present arrangement allowed Clive to flourish, and the food proved to be exceptional.

Having survived the journey north, Neil remembers how, once he had enjoyed a decent cup of tea (Taylors of Harrogate), feelings of nervousness returned as he prepared for his initial reconnaissance of Bakewell. Three years previously such moments had presaged experiences he thrived on: arriving at an unknown place, those first perambulations, exploring and uncovering. But he had undertaken those adventures in very different circumstances - and with his camera riding shotgun. As he stepped out into a weak winter sun, the latter remained encased in its temporary home at the bottom of his room's wardrobe.

That first excursion, brief but adequate, had been sufficient to put Neil's mind at rest; Bakewell was hardly alien territory. He eked out a small loop involving the Bath Gardens, windows of various Bakewell Tart shops, the old bridge, then through the market square to the River Wye, one of its footbridges adorned with 'love padlocks' in copy-cat homage to the Pont des Arts in Paris. He picked up leaflets from the tourist office, including one for the Monsal Trail which started up at the old station and which, Abi later assured him, was worth a stroll if he was a walking kind of a person. He wasn't really, but it felt like something to try, perhaps on Christmas Day, an excursion for the Canon. When she had asked him about his work, part of a standard opening gambit for all her guests he assumed, he had been a little vague: "I've been working for some magazines", which seemed to prove acceptable enough. And the reason he was in Bakewell on his own at Christmas? "Just to get away, really. There have been some changes in personal circumstances. Clearing the mind; that sort of thing." Able to relate to such motivation, she had nodded, giving the impression that what was likely to be driving him was the best reason in the world for doing absolutely anything - or absolutely nothing, depending on your perspective.

When he lifted his camera from its case the following morning it felt strangely unfamiliar. His plan was simple enough: having briefly established the lie of the land the previous day, to walk back into town and take some photographs; nothing rushed or special. He wanted to hold the Canon out in the open again, to take shots that weren't demanded of him because of a contract, that didn't rely on artificial lighting or provocative nudity. It was to be, in its own way, a reacquaintance. With something of a stab, he realised had taken no photographs on his own terms, for his own purposes, for months. He had become so absorbed in framing the girls, teasing the best - the most seductive! - out of them, that he had ignored the core of his professional ambition. Indeed, what of it was left? Perhaps this abandonment had been part of the reason for the distance that had grown between himself and Cath; perhaps his withdrawal from more mainstream photography in preference for the superficial, the trite, the commercial, had bled into his domestic life. What had she said? "I though you were serious." It is easy for him to make this analysis sitting on Parliament Hill, separated from Bakewell by a hundred-and-fifty miles and five years, spying on himself that Christmas Eve morning as he sat in his room's comfy chair, checking his lenses for dust, his batteries for power. But at the time?

Breakfast - as with dinner the previous evening - proved to be exceptionally good. Clive's food was perfectly cooked, each item clean, distinct, avoiding the trap into which some hotel breakfasts can fall where components appear discrete on the plate yet all manage to end up tasting the same. The bread for the toast had been generously sliced, the tea good and strong. It was as he supposed all breakfasts should be: fortifying and sufficiently enlivening to allow him to push on through the checking of his equipment, then to re-bag it, finish his ablutions, and head out.

By ten-thirty the streets were already surprisingly lively, bustling with people going about their 'last-minute' business: the acquiring of food or wine; the panicked hunt for those slippers and other presents they had somehow forgotten to buy; parents helping children to spend their pocket money on little tokens for Daddy or Mummy rather than waste it on extra bags of Haribos. More than once as he navigated toward the Bath Gardens he heard echoes of "Let's wait and see what Santa brings, shall we?". Back at the flat there were no presents to give, none to unwrap; in that respect Christmas was a blank.

He had settled on the gardens as a safe place to start. Yes, they were largely denuded of colour, the brown of the soil punctuated here and there by the odd splash of evergreen and the largely hidden promise of the Spring to come, but as an ensemble it had the clear advantage of being radically different from what he had been shooting recently. He found he didn't want to have to compare, and in a way the muted tones seemed appropriate with which to begin his re-education. Of course, he knew the photographs he would take were likely to be disappointing, after all, he was completely out of practice with any kind of 'landscape'; but as he sat on one of the garden's benches he tried to tell himself that this time it really didn't matter.

Not wanting to stand out too much - to create an image which announced to anyone who happened to be passing that he was 'a photographer' - he chose a mid-range telephoto lens so that he could take shots from where he sat, and began with simple zoomed-in compositions of the virtually naked herbaceous borders. They offered little real intrinsic interest and minimal opportunities to be creative, but it was a start. After twenty or so shots, the sound of outdoor shutter-clicks began to edge him towards the historically familiar.

There was a path through the centre of the gardens leading from the main thoroughfare to a minor road on its northern edge. Given the general populous were likely to be preoccupied with 'last-minute Christmas', Neil expected to have the gardens more or less to himself, and yet there was a steady stream of pedestrians using the path to make the journey between the central A6-A619 roundabout and the quiet of Bath Street. More than once he had to wait for people to pass before pressing the shutter release. He only noticed the signs attached to the park railings - 'Xmas Fair' - after about five minutes, a bold black arrow pointing away from the heart of the town and through the gardens. Which explained the human traffic. For a while he sat, camera cradled on his lap, and watched people as they went by, each displaying various mixes of purpose, urgency, and desperation. From the looks on their faces he tried to decipher who they were and the mission upon which they were engaged: a husband heading to the fair to try and find something for his wife, perhaps; a woman with her children on their way back into town, she cradling a simple unmarked paper carrier bag, a present for Daddy maybe; an elderly couple looking worn-out, hopefully on their way home.

Sheltering in thick coats, scarves, hats, gloves, you could tell nothing about these people except from what was displayed on their faces, and he suddenly recalled the corridor in the hospital and the photographs of the staff adorning the walls there. Shocked to be thrown back in time nearly two months, he found himself unable to prevent the resurgence of memory, powerless to stop his mind from dredging the recent past. Those horrible hours came to him as if in a painting, cubist at best, abstract at worst. He saw the blue door of the room in which Cath lay; imagined the neon-like red and green flashing numbers on the monitors; repainted the white and pink of the staff attire. They were images strangely filled with colour - and disturbingly without emotion. If at the time, sitting in Bath Gardens, he attributed such an absence to his having exhausted all feelings about that night, he would find out soon enough that he had not. But above all else, at that precise moment - just after eleven a.m. on Christmas Eve in a grey Derbyshire public garden - what came back to him most powerfully were the black-and-white portraits of the NHS workers. Not uppermost in his mind because of who they were and what they did, nor because they or people like them had tried to save Cath's life, but because of what they represented: unadulterated images of honest people. Again unbidden, he recalled Rico's comments about taking portraits and 'trust', and thought of the kind of photographs with which he had been engaged for months. They shared none of the attributes of those staff images: his were garishly coloured, completely staged, and in probably more than one sense, undeniably manipulated. They were dishonest.

He had spent over a year fabricating fantasies. At a profound level he had been lying both to the girls themselves and the magazine buyers who ended up viewing the photographs he had taken. Worse than that, he had lied to himself. And he had lied to Cath. That knowledge, undeniable and sudden, hit him as hard as anything ever had; a powerful and shocking blow to his mental solar plexus. Feeling his body sag, he almost dropped his camera, only to be roused by someone wishing him "Merry Christmas" as they passed, a greeting immediately followed by the sound of a car horn from the roundabout. Unaware he had been sitting head bowed, he looked up again to locate the well-wisher - an elderly lady on her way through to Bath Street - and became instantly cognisant of some moisture in his right eye which he ascribed to the cold wind as he wiped it away with his sleeve.

Was this what he had to do? Did he need to subject himself to some kind of exorcism in order to find his way? He thought of what Harry had said, and trotted out the platitudes to which others might all too readily resort - like "pull yourself together!" - and he sensed they would be correct, in spirit at least. Whatever happened now was down to him; his next move, the next thing he said, even the next photograph he took. Had he been a religious person he might have reached a different conclusion. And the one scene that was to prove difficult to shift, a constant through those brief moments of examination and for some while after, the one which soon came to feel as if it had lasted a lifetime already, was that of the hospital corridor.

Suddenly shivering, he placed his camera back into its bag and stood up, pulling his scarf closer about his neck, his collar slightly higher. He thought about going through to the Xmas Fair but chose not to, unable to conjure any valid reason for doing so. Walking out of the gardens' main entrance, he turned left and headed through the busy streets to the stone road bridge where made his way down onto the path that ran along the river and thus to begin his loop back to the hotel. It was marginally quieter here, but the people who passed him all displayed the tell-tale signs of Christmas, whether they were struggling with multiple bags or giving off an aura of holiday and festivities. Perhaps there were more smiles on faces than there would normally be.

It was busier by the shallow weir, more a step in the river bed than anything else. Of the two structures that joined the town to the car parks on the other side of the river, on the bridge with the padlocks the pedestrian flow was more dense, the movement constant, giving him a sense of disorganised community, but community nonetheless. Resisting the temptation to follow the herd into the main shopping area, he continued along the side of the river a little further and towards the second crossing. He could see that one was also busy, but less so, and about mid-distance between the two there seemed a mini oasis of calm populated with fewer people. Finding an unoccupied bench, Neil sat once more and looked up and down the river.

From this distance he could see there were two types of traffic on the lock bridge: the first were those on a mission, hurrying to and from cars, either laden or soon to be so; the second were the complete opposite, in no apparent hurry at all, taking their time to look at the river, the ducks swimming in it, and the locks attached to the railings. He pulled out his camera once more. If anyone paid any attention to him he was fairly confident they would assume he was taking photographs of the water, the ducks paddling back and forth; how could they have possibly known he had moved to a lens that was powerful enough to get close-ups of the pedestrians on the bridge? He concentrated on people who appeared to be just looking, catching them as they bent to the metal uprights, fingering the chunks of metal fixed to them. They seemed to be drawn to the larger and more colourful padlocks, and where things had been written, were trying to make out what had been inscribed. He imagined, somewhat uncharitably, 'Darren loves Kasey' or 'BH 4 SC'.

Using the viewfinder to pan along the bridge, his movement was arrested by an elderly couple who were standing virtually motionless. They were not waiting for anyone to let them pass, but they were nevertheless intent on something, their eyes transfixed. He clicked the shutter release then zoomed out slightly to see if he could identify the object of their attention. Slightly ahead of them, separated by about two metres, a young couple were bent at the railings. At first Neil assumed they were examining the padlocks as others were, but as he looked it became evident that they were adding their own testament to the collection. Their fingers merging together as they fastened and tested the link, he clicked more rapidly, a few shots capturing both couples, hopefully framing the image like bookends. Then, as the young couple stood, he closed in on them, filling the frame. He could see they had a key in their hands; both had fingers on it as they moved it above the railings and out over the water. Quickly he panned out once more to include the elderly couple again, then zoomed back in, as closely as he could on the younger pair, their hands, the key. Shooting as if it were an action sequence, he could only hope he had captured the moment when they released the key to the water - as well as those afterwards when they looked down to try and find it nestled amongst all the rest. The young man put his arm around the girl. She looked up and kissed him as if to say "well, that's that then". The elderly couple - looking slightly embarrassed as if they had intruded on something special and private - began to move, heading towards the shops. As he put down his camera, for the first time in a long while he suddenly felt keen to check the images newly secured within his Canon. He hoped they were good.

The vibration of his phone pulls Neil out of his reverie. As he retrieves it from his pocket he sees again the city, another plane on its descent. It is almost as if he has just arrived on the hill and not been sitting there for over half-an-hour. The text message shines out at him.

SORRY. TRAFFIC AWFUL. WILL BE A FEW MINUTES LATE. X

He had suggested to Beth that she park near his house and walk up to Parliament Hill to join him. She had briefly questioned the sense of doing that rather than simply meet him at his home, but his claim that he wanted to take some photographs proved, under the circumstances, to be the only excuse he needed.

He stared at the single 'x' and wondered how far along the journey towards a lock and its key he might now be.

❖

"We have something of a tradition," Abi said at breakfast the following morning as she delivered his toast to the table, "of sharing our Christmas meal with our guests, if that's acceptable to you."

It was said in a manner which suggested there could be no other possible outcome, and Neil found himself wondering what she would have been like to work with in the City. 'Spiky' he suspected.

"That would be very nice."

"There are three of you - and of course Clive and I. Seven o'clock?"

"Given Clive's cooking, I wouldn't miss it for the world."

She smiled, finding the compliment perfectly appropriate.

"Any plans for today?"

"I thought I might drive up to the Monsal Trail car park and go for a walk."

"That's a splendid idea," Abi concurred. "If it wasn't Christmas Day I'd suggest hiring a bike; but walking's just as good. Head towards the viaduct; that and the tunnel before it is always rewarding the first time someone sees it."

As it had been with the town the previous day, the bustle of the car park surprised him; perhaps he had been a little naïve to expect to have the trail to himself on Christmas morning. Once he had interrogated an information board at the old station, he headed off - though not yet entirely settled on the twelve kilometre round trip to Monsal Head. After a short while he found his stride and began to relax, his camera bag pressing reassuringly down on his right shoulder. He found it relatively easy to categorise the trail's other users, all seemingly bolstered by an exaggeration of yuletide bonhomie. First there were the dog walkers, people who were taking their pets for what appeared to be a regular constitution; they exhibited a certain familiarity with their surroundings, an impression enhanced by a total lack of concern about the precise location of their animals once freed from their leashes as if their going off into adjacent fields and eventually coming back at a different point on the walk were par for the course. Then there were the cyclists. These seemed to fall into two camps: the hardened, lycra-clad brigade in their Tour de France replica gear, and the families, many of whom seemed to boast children stress-testing for the first time what could only be presents dropped off by Santa overnight. The third group consisted of everyone else, people just out for a walk. The majority were couples, though there were a few larger groups. Singletons were in the minority and for a while he felt as if he stood out more than anyone else.

When he reached Hassop, Neil paused to free his Canon from its bag, replacing the lens he had been using the previous day with a standard 55mm non-zoom, and then preoccupied himself over the next few kilometres with snapshots of bridges, vistas of rolling fields, and old station platforms. By the time he reached Headstone Tunnel he was just about ready to turn around, but the photographic lure of the long stretch of darkness ahead of him with its promise of light at the far end was too much to resist and so he carried on, eventually emerging under an open sky at the Monsal Head viaduct. Like many of his fellow walkers, he snapped dutifully where he was supposed to - though almost everyone else was using their phones - and leaned on the viaduct wall to peer down into the Monsal valley. Before he started back he switched back to the previous day's zoom 'just in case'.

"How was your walk?" Preparations for dinner obviously perfectly under control, it was Clive who offered him a drink when he walked into the dining room a little before seven.

"Splendid. Took a little longer than I expected, and it was busy too, but good all the same."

"It's very popular," Clive passed him a gin and tonic. "You have to know when to go."

Already there, the two other guests were talking to Abi who wasted no time in beckoning Neil over to make the formal introductions. Michael was late middle-aged - Neil guessed around sixty-eight - who confessed he had been a Christmas regular there for about seven years, ever since he lost his wife to cancer. "That first Christmas I had to get away, you know? Finding Abi and Clive was a Godsend, and I've been coming back ever since. It's like an annual treat." For a brief moment Neil struggled with the abstract notion that he too might end up like Michael, a regular returnee; but he had thirty years on the elder man and so much more living to do - a thought simultaneously both warming and daunting.

About ten years older than he, Deborah - "my friends call me Debs!" - had, like Neil, arrived on the off-chance, her motivation confessed as being "to clear my head, now that I've rid myself of my foul ex-husband". Neil mused how an observer might be forgiven for regarding them as a rather sad triumvirate; a trio who, in their own particular ways, were either running away or hiding from something - not that was how he would have chosen to see himself. Perhaps he had been softened by the bracing walk and the general sense of companionship made all the more pervasive thanks to the subtle glue Abi and Clive applied, but he found it difficult not to take a liking to both Debs and Michael, fellow pilgrims who were trying to find something to replace what they had lost.

"And what do you do, Neil?"

They had been between courses, taking a rest after a splendid roast goose - "one of Clive's specialties!" - and before embarking on what Michael assured him would be the best Christmas pudding he had ever tasted.

It was a question he knew would surface at some point or another. Michael and Debs having taken turns to be the focal point for a few minutes, the latter now turned to him. From the side, Abi skilfully pulled almost invisible conversational threads. Because he had known it would be asked, he had already decided how he would answer it.

"I'm a photographer," he said, spoken as if he were trying the words on for size.

"Really?!"

"Oh, nothing too notable. Magazines, mainly. I've done a few things for Condé Nast, for example."

"That sounds exciting," said Debs, "don't they send you to all sorts of exotic places?"

Neil offered a short summary of the more interesting commissions he had undertaken, a move which allowed the conversation to broaden out to travel in general and the five of them to embark on a gentle game of oneupmanship typical of such gatherings, each exchanging romanticised highlights of some of the places they had visited. When Clive rose to go to the kitchen to bring through the pudding, Neil's companionable conclusion was that the contest had more or less ended in a draw.

*

If it all feels like ancient history as he sits basking in the warmth of a cloudless London day, then it is not just the different season and the passage of years that makes it so. Neil knows the person who sat at the dinner table that evening was not the person he is now; rather he regards him as an earlier incarnation of himself, a 'Mark 1' - or more likely a 'Mark 2'. It is a reconnection without any real affection or attachment. That Christmas he had been at the beginning of a transition, a stage through which he'd had to go to become the man he is today. Cath had provided the bookends for the version of himself he was destined to leave behind after Bakewell, but how many journeys had he been on since then? And now there was another in the offing.

The Boxing Day journey back to London had, in many ways, been diametrically opposed to the trek north just three days earlier: he had been returning with something to look forward to - the interrogation of the photographs captured in his camera. That stirring of excitement was a new old-feeling, however tepid it might have been. And he found he travelled with company; the images from the hospital corridor, once resurrected, had begun to haunt him like a friendly ghost. Yet there had been some trepidation in his return too. Not in the going back to the city, but in reengaging with the flat, stepping into the major relic of his old life. He hadn't thought that much about it, not in any focussed way, but as he retraced his steps, coming off the M1 and heading ever closer to the apartment, the sense of another decision needing to be made grew increasingly acute.

It proved to be a case of one thing at a time - and both flat and photographs were trumped by a domestic imperative as soon as he walked through the door. Whether it was a mechanism to delay tackling either, Neil threw himself into a frenzy of the pragmatic: working his way through two lots of washing; changing his bedding and putting out fresh towels; culling the fridge and cupboards of out-of-date produce; putting together a shopping list for the supermarket in the morning; working out what he was going to eat that evening. He smiles as he recalls those couple of hours, not because they were intrinsically funny, but because they would have felt alien to the person who had so recently walked out of the flat not really caring if he ever saw it again. It might have been a sign. Only after that burst of activity - almost literally 'wiping the slate clean' - did he switch on his computer, plug in his camera, and allow the images to download while he prepared the last ready-meal he had found in the freezer. 'Cook from frozen'.

After the luxury of Clive's cooking, nothing he could prepare for himself was ever going to come close, let alone a derivative dish pulled from a supermarket chiller; yet although the Biriani was bland and uninspiring, it proved acceptable as an accompaniment to the main course - scanning through his Bakewell photographs.

As he suspected, the ones he had taken in Bath Gardens were predominately dull; although hampered by the lack of colour, they were fundamentally undone by unimaginative composition. Of those he had surreptitiously taken of individuals passing through, one or two showed limited promise. Wishing to get all the disappointment out of the way in one go - and partially distracted anyway in finishing the remnants of his meal - he skipped on to those taken on the Monsal Trail. It was a similar story except for a very small number around the tunnel, particularly one where he had managed to capture a dog urinating against the wall at the tunnel mouth, the stark black contrast of what lay beyond juxtaposed against the dog's indifference. "Another pissing dog!" he thought, and for a moment he was back in Sienna, perhaps the point when everything truly started.

Finishing his last forkful of rice, he rose and walked the plate through to the kitchen, taking the opportunity to refresh his glass with another beer. Over his shoulder he sensed the screen waiting for him, the cursor poised, pointing, ready to be called into action. He had been suddenly nervous. Although on reflection the next few minutes had proven momentous in their own way, it is another memory that makes him smile, because now he can afford to do so - and because there might have been other, more problematic outcomes.

There were a total of forty-two shots of people on the bridge, a large proportion of these taken in the burst when the young couple were dropping their key into the river. Of all these photographs, three subjects stood out: the elderly couple transfixed by the scene before them - both in isolation and then in a composition with the lock-fasteners; the lovers as they attached the lock itself; and the moment the key was dropped, where Neil had zoomed in on their hands. There was a balance about these in that they offered three alternative views of the same event, three different styles of composition, three different intensities of zoom. It took him very little time to dismiss all the other images, and this allowed him to concentrate on finding the best examples for each of the trio. Where the two couples bookended the frame, a pair at either edge of the shot, in one instance he had been lucky that at the precise moment he had pressed the shutter release, the space between them had become clear, uncompromised by others walking by. Given how busy it had been on the bridge, this had been pure fluke. He thought back to the Sienna photograph again.

Having chosen the best of those 'long shots', he then concentrated on the young couple working at the lock. With their heads bent to their task, their faces were partially obscured, and this led the viewer to focus on what they were doing rather than who they were. There was one image, taken just as they were about to withdraw the key, which seemed to sum up the moment perfectly, their fingers intertwined to such an extent that it seemed almost impossible to tell which digits belonged to which person.

However, the most magical of the entire suite were the eleven rapid-fire close-up shots he had taken just as they were releasing the key. These were all about the hands, the key, and the relationship between the two. In the first of them, the key was still in their possession; in the last, it had already travelled perhaps six inches on it's journey into the water below. As he sipped his beer, Neil tried to choose the distance between fingers and key where the pictorial magic happened. He settled on about an inch; close enough to still have some tentative link to their hands, but far enough away for that bond to have been broken and the die cast. No going back. He finds himself wondering whether he and Cath would have fixed a lock to a bridge railing as a symbol of their love - and thrown away its key as a statement of its permanence. If he suspects not, he is unsure if it is opinion informed by the passage of events.

By the time he reached the bottom of his glass he had settled on just four photographs from his Bakewell sojourn: those three from the bridge and the dog at the tunnel mouth. Having arranged them so that he could see all four simultaneously, each one taking up a quarter of his screen, he leaned back in his chair to take them in as a group, to try and assess them. He found himself not only interested in their quality as images, but also in the far more nebulous value of 'worth'. Had he known what he was looking for? Had any of this creative activity been premeditated? To a limited degree only. Sitting on his Parliament Hill bench looking out onto the city and back into the past, he sees that evening for what it was: that earlier version of himself scrabbling about in the fog looking for a way out. Or a man thrown overboard praying for a life raft.

They did have worth, and in the same way his ghosts from the hospital had worth; they were genuine, honest, unadulterated. They hinted at more than what you could see on the surface. The parallel spurred him to further action. He made copies of the four images and converted them all to black-and-white, his aim to remove distraction, to hone in on what mattered. It was hardly a master-stroke, but they became even more powerful, what they spoke about all the more profound. Was it a road to

129

Damascus moment? He didn't believe in such things, but he shivered all the same. Without needing to recall any of them to the screen, he thought of all the shots he had been taking for the best part of the last two years. They were completely the opposite: garish, manufactured, shallow. All surface and no substance.

Was that what he had become too - and if so, was that the cause of him losing more than just his photographic soul? The quartet he was looking at suddenly represented the sort of photos he wanted to take; the photos that said something about *him*. In all the shots of the girls he was nowhere, only inserting himself into the narrative in a very real and physical way after his camera had been put away. First and foremost he had betrayed himself, and in doing so perhaps the outcome and its knock-on effects were inevitable.

As he watches a couple stroll past him - a couple remarkably similar to the young people on the bridge - he tries to recall if that was the moment he had cried, for himself, for Cath. There had been one such episode and he had been alone in his flat when it happened. Had that Boxing Day session reviewing his output from Bakewell been the catalyst? In a way he knows it doesn't really matter. What does matter is that he did cry at some point (and if not then, soon after), and that the exercise started that evening provided him with a sufficient level of recognition to gift him the opportunity to move on. Consciously or not, Neil knows at that precise moment he had made a decision which would affect his working future, and that he had reset the bar - and set it incredibly high.

The following morning he set out early for the supermarket, joining the throng for whom, it seemed, Christmas and Boxing Days had completely denuded their kitchen cupboards generating the need for yet another mass stocking-up session. In spite of that, it proved something of a cathartic and strangely enjoyable experience, one he soon moulded into a weekly routine. It was satisfying to get that part of his life reigned in and under control; one less thing he didn't really have to think about too much. Which was welcome given what was left to resolve.

Conscious he still needed to arrive at a conclusion on the flat - a dilemma initially left to be worked on by his subconscious like a computer processing a job in the background - just after eleven o'clock found him sitting once again in front of his Mac, this time armed with no more than coffee and two Florentines (a luxury to which he had been introduced by Abi and Clive). His first move was to start where he had left off the previous evening, filling his screen with his four best Bakewell images (their black-and-white versions) in order to see how he felt about them a little over twelve hours later. And as it turned out, he felt even more enthusiasm for them - or perhaps that was a knock-on effect of the chocolatey biscuits! Yet if these pictures represented a marker-post for his future, a lay-line to provide him guidance, then what was his next move? And if he was setting himself a challenge - that new, super-high bar to which he should aspire - then what did that mean for all his work to-date, not merely over the previous two years, but for every single photograph he had ever taken? Neil instinctively knew there could be no partial reset.

Forcing himself into action, he created a empty folder on his hard drive and copied the four new images into it. A start. He had decided to build a new portfolio based on strict criteria of worth and honesty; and although he knew he could never define precisely what those things meant, he had to trust himself to be rigorous in what qualified and what did not. In a way, the whole notion of 'honesty' actually started with himself. And so, across the next three days, he reviewed every single photograph in his enormous collection, weighing it against the new standard he had set; if a photograph appeared likely to meet that stringent criteria, he converted it to black-and-white and assessed it again.

If it was still in the running for promotion, he moved it into a folder where he had decided to store 'shortlisted' material. On New Year's Eve afternoon, he prepared for the advancing of the year by going through all those contenders once more, the select few finally being dropped into his new portfolio. He wanted only those which he could defend, not simply from the nebulous consideration of 'worth' and 'honesty', but because he knew they said something else, spoke beyond the image, carried a message or a story. Even said something about him. He would only include those he felt proud to have taken - and which, given the opportunity, he would take again, and in exactly the same way.

When he stood up from his desk in the early evening to go and prepare his dinner, he did so believing he had done the best job possible. He had been ruthless and maintained his focus throughout, assuring himself that not for one instant had he taken the easy option, never approving an image because it was really difficult to make the binary decision, fighting those impulses when just saying 'yes' was the easy way out, a compromise which allowed him to advance to the next photo. Indeed, his default was if he was unsure then it had to a rejected. The result, after all those hours of study and effort, was an incredibly small selection: the Sienna dog; one of Cath as she posed dramatically that first day they met; a couple from the Edinburgh shoot; just three from all his other Condé Nast commissions; Sophie on the balcony; the four from Bakewell. Only a dozen - and not even a Baker's Dozen. If it seemed scant reward for years of endeavour, Neil chose not to look at it that way. Rather, he preferred to see it as a solid platform upon which to build his future. Road to Damascus indeed.

And all the while he had been working at his collection, in the background the question of the flat was being analysed in readiness for his giving it some undivided attention. That came after dinner. It seemed only right and proper that he should start the new year with the 'big questions' answered, without putting anything off. Perhaps this was all about honesty and worth too, in it's own way.

It was another binary choice: to stay or to move. There was a purely emotional answer, of course, but Neil had determined not to rush to that; if it were a decision with which he then had to live - and how could it not be?! - then he needed all the justification he could lay his hands on.

In terms of his current abode, there was little wrong with it. It was perhaps slightly larger than he needed, but the prospect of downsizing did not score highly. That seemed to suggest a point in favour of staying, as did avoiding the hassle of both house-hunting then moving. But those were the 'easy' choices, akin to the approach he had deliberated eschewed when it came to his photographs. If he did remain in situ, then he could always change the character of the place by seeking to redecorate, get in some new furniture, rearranging things. It was, on the whole, a low-risk approach. One counter-argument could have been expense. Ralph had been subsidising them of course, and though that subsidy had now been withdrawn, Neil wondered if he had yet to truly grasp its impact. Indeed, his finances had the potential to be a significant spoiler; they would, for example, undoubtedly prevent him from scaling *up*. Whether or not she had contemplated changing it, Cath had left everything to him in her will which meant that, in addition to the savings pot into which they had both contributed - the money set aside to deliver her dream - he also inherited a significant sum about which he had been unaware. Perhaps it had been some kind of 'dowry' from her father, or something she had been gifted when she reached eighteen or twenty-one; whatever the source, it was now very firmly his. When he initially found out about it, he had considered speaking to Ralph for guidance, but given her father had never asked after the money - and had quite deliberately and pointedly severed all ties with him - Neil ceased to concern himself about it. He knew doing so might be construed as callous or selfish or cold-hearted, but the money sat in one of his accounts and was his to do with as he wished. So money was not really a factor in deciding the fate of the flat - though there were obviously longer-term considerations on that front.

All of which brought him back to his emotional response and what proved to be the trump card. Neil's eventual decision was driven by time: what he wanted for the future, and his relationship to the past. No matter how much he might decorate and remodel its contents, the flat would still be the home he shared with Cath; he had never lived there on his own. No amount of 'silk sheen' Dulux could change that. He knew that history would be a spectre never far from his shoulder, present every time he turned on the cooker, ran a bath, opened a window. And if the exercise he had been through with his photographs had been about setting a new direction for the future, then it seemed right that he should shift domestically too. A fresh start on all fronts; a new Neil.

So, he would move.

Saying and doing were two different things, of course, and a need to revalidate his financial position in the light of this decision dug him in the ribs. He played with some numbers on a spreadsheet, modelling budgets for a new flat, the likely cost of moving; and then tried to factor in living expenses to see how the whole bundle would affect his store of cash. It was unlikely to dissipate overnight, but dwindle away it would - especially if he had nothing coming in. Work of some kind was, he knew, inevitable. But not Rico's kind of work. It would not need to be constant, merely sufficient to keep his coffers in a healthy state; and it should not be so time-consuming that he found himself unable to devote time to working on his new portfolio. He believed he could keep the two threads separate - after all, to some extent he had been able to mask one life from another for the last two years. Didn't he have some practice in managing duplicity? With that in mind, he drew up a list of contacts who might be able to put work his way - including Condé Nast - and drafted a letter informing them that he was getting "back behind the camera" (a phrase he would change twenty-four hours later!) and once again available for commissions, however small.

"You're quite sure?" Rico's voice had treacled toward him from his mobile phone two days later.

Neil had decided the least he could do was to inform him directly. Suggesting a meeting in their usual Soho haunt had been his first instinct, but he knew how persuasive Rico could be face-to-face, and, given he was in the very earliest stages of reinventing himself, remained unsure just how strong the 'new' Neil might be.

"New Year, new me. Isn't that what they say? I think I owe it to myself to start over."

"Back to basics?"

"Something like that."

There was a short pause.

"Well look, Neil. You're one of the best, okay? I can't say I'm surprised, though I am disappointed. But if you ever need to earn a few quid - just as a one-off or something - you know where I am. When I tell some of the girls I'm sure they'll be heart-broken; I bet one or two of them will want me to persuade you to change your mind."

"Which would be nice of them," he laughed softly. "In any event, give them my love. Maybe I'll see them around, or on another shoot another day. Who knows?"

❋

As those few days come flooding back to him, he conjures an image to fit the process upon which he had embarked. Looking down on London now, he feels as if he had taken a snapshot of the city, removed all colour from it, then traced lines around its component parts so that it resembled a complex paint-by-numbers canvas. The task he had set himself was to start filling in the blanks, to reimagine the city and his life. Perhaps the decision about the future direction of his photography succeeded in shading one shape - large rather than small, he assumed - and the one relating to the flat blocked out another. How many had he addressed in those first few days? As he scans the familiar vista, he is of course unable to say; it is as impossible to articulate that as it is to know how many of those imagined shapes he has filled-in over the five years since then. A few? Most? Certainly not all. And has he, on occasion, strayed over the boundaries of a shape, bleeding into another? Given how things are connected, that is surely the case. He imagines himself sitting there, brush in hand; in less than an hour he will have tackled another segment. Small or large, he doesn't yet know; and as for colour..?

But colour had been something essentially banished from his life as that year ticked over. He had determined his serious photography would be all black-and-white, and already had an inkling that people rather than landscape would play the leading role. Less overtly, he had also decided he would live a black-and-white kind of life, keeping it simple, regulated almost. The weekly supermarket shop was a somewhat mundane example of this, demoting the essentially irrelevant and aligning it with his overarching desire to pursue honesty. There was something clear-cut about being straight with himself and others; consciously or not, he wanted to try and avoid 'shades'.

The city had its part to play too. Somewhere ahead of him, couched amongst the roofs and trees, Kentish Town and their old flat. Behind him on the other side of the hill, Hampstead, where he lived now. On the first of January, once he had decided to move, had he any idea in which part of the city he might land? There were some preferences he possessed that remain with him still: an affinity for north of the river; a predilection to not stray too far from the Heath; and some more obscure areas of bias, such as a fondness for the Northern Line. If the latter were to be his guide, then it suggested somewhere like Tufnell Park or Highgate to the east, or Chalk Farm, Belsize Park or even Hampstead itself to the west. If it had been a narrow enough geography for his initial consideration, settling on the western leg of the line sharpened the focus further. Of course this time there was no Ralph pulling strings in the background, and he had to resort to mundane detective work and hope for old-fashioned luck. Having registered with some letting agencies more out of hope than expectation, he remembers being surprised when one actually rang him out of the blue a few days later about a top floor conversion not that far from Belsize Park tube. It had been an agent he had never heard of, but one recommended by Rico - so perhaps there had been forces at work in the background even then. As chance would have it, a prospective tenant had been forced to pull out at the last minute after a job offer had fallen through and Neil was being given first refusal if he could move quickly. He had been at the property within forty minutes, decided to take it five minutes after that, and had signed the papers by the end of the next day. Lucky indeed.

It had been slightly smaller than the Kentish Town flat - and slightly more expensive. After verbally committing to the tenancy, he remembered returning to his spreadsheet to ensure he hadn't done anything that would greatly compromise his financial future. He found he might need one or two more pieces of work to cover himself, but was reassured he should be fine. He smiles to himself, instinctively glancing away to his right and to where, similarly hidden, that new flat had been located. If moving there had been the result of having made a conscious choice, then it would have been an inspired one; but Neil knows he had no real say in the matter. If he hadn't taken it, how much longer might he have needed to wait before the next opportunity arose? With things in the property market moving at their typical breakneck London speed, he was installed in Belsize Park before the end of the month, and thus able to embark on the process of filing the Kentish Town flat into memory.

Paid work came slowly. The first call he had in mid-February comes back to him as clearly as if it had been yesterday. In itself, it hadn't been the nature of the work that was significant, but rather what it represented; he had thought of it as stepping onto the first rung of new ladder. Not the professional ladder where it mattered - that was to be rooted in his new portfolio, the talisman of his new ambition - but rather the pragmatic, commercial one; the ladder he needed to be on in order to survive financially, to give himself the freedom to concentrate where he really wanted. A friend-of-a-friend was looking for someone to undertake a house shoot for one of the homes-and-gardens publications that were becoming increasingly popular. They had been given his name and had seen some of his old Condé Nast work. The property was located in the very south of Derbyshire where they had just had significant snowfall; the house was looking magical in the landscape, he was told, and the owner didn't want to miss the 'fairy tale' opportunity. The photographer the magazine had booked had gone off with 'flu. Was he interested? They were sorry that it was short notice, but could he do tomorrow? They'd pick him up at seven.

In many respects it was a perfect assignment: he didn't care about it emotionally; there were no people involved; he was highly unlikely to confuse the gig - in terms of motivation or output - with where he had set his sights, that still nebulous and vaguely defined goal. Looking back he wonders if he may have wavered slightly when he first saw the house, his mind translating the stunning vista - all that snow! - into a black-and-white image that would have looked great as a poster on a wall. Once inside, the owners of the property - an ex-City trader and his ex-actress wife - gave him a tour of the house and told him what they wanted the magazine to showcase. He tried to understand their reasoning, their motivation behind opening up their home like this. They had both spent their lives showing off one way or another, and perhaps this was simply an extension of that. He recalls slipping into 'photographer mode', readying his equipment, and then moving room-to-room with his cameras and a small but powerful portable spotlight for filling-in. The woman trailed around with him, asking questions, making suggestions; Neil used her to switch lights on and off, to rearrange cushions and temporarily remove anything that looked less than photogenic - which wasn't, in the end, very much at all. When he had finished, they fed and watered him while he waited for his lift back to town, asking him about his work; he leant on his experience in exhibitions and with Condé Nast shoots. Safe territory; people were always interested in those.

Much of the next day was spent going through the selection and editing process. He found it refreshing that he could detach himself from it, approach the photographs with a purely objective eye. Having been asked for four shots of each room from which the magazine would choose, he provided six; it was important not to mess-up this first assignment. Creating the right impression was, he knew all too well, fundamental. They seemed happy enough, and when the article was eventually published a few weeks later, he was pleased with how it looked; the shots were crisp and clean, the house looked stunning. The owners sent him a bottle of wine with a note of thanks.

When he drank the wine he toasted not the output of the shoot nor the quality of the photographs he had taken, but himself - and the fact that he had proved he could still undertake a 'normal' assignment, one which didn't involve naked young women spreading their legs or pointing their breasts at the camera. Obtusely, he also celebrated his success for being detached, *un*invested in the end result other than at the level of the images themselves. The most important thing was that he had begun to demonstrate that it could be possible to have a foot on both ladders - the personal and the pragmatic - and to keep them separate from one and other. At the most basic of levels, it had been the successful execution of a photographic contract. The ex-City wheeler-dealer owner of the Derbyshire house would surely have approved.

During that February and March, as commissions for work began to dribble in slowly but adequately - some advertising work, a follow-up 'homes' shoot, and bizarrely some photographs of new models of touring coaches - Neil recalls his initial struggle with the more serious activity. Having decided people should be at the heart of his new oeuvre, the first objective he set himself was to go and capture some. Given there were people everywhere he looked, it sounded the kind of task that should have been easy to fulfil. He had, however, found himself wrestling with where to find his source material. At first glance it would appear all too easy to take photographs of people - for example now, as he sits on the bench watching them walk past him, central London providing the backdrop. But he discovered very quickly that, unlike Rico's models, average people going about their daily business simply don't like being photographed. If they see someone with a camera pointed in their direction, the majority become very defensive.

His first experiment had been with volume. He would go into town and locate himself at a popular thoroughfare and simply take shots of people passing. What could be easier? He chose Trafalgar Square, Oxford Circus, the pedestrian bridge over the river by Tate Britain. But when he aimed his camera at anyone who appeared moderately interesting - making somewhat arbitrary selections from the throng - other than the few extroverts who would adopt an exaggerated pose, most would turn away or put their heads down. This was especially the case at the Bankside bridge where they had no alternate route; they simply had to walk past him. Occasionally one or two were openly hostile towards him. A man with a camera was not to be trusted. To compensate he tried using a tripod and a remote trigger, setting the camera to focus on a particular location - such as a point on the National Gallery steps - and, standing away from the device, pressed the release as casually as he could manage just as his target should have been coming into shot. This allowed him to take photographs of people who were not shying away from him - and therefore also unlikely to accost him - but often they ended up inadequately framed, and when he examined them later found himself awash with people in coats, scarves and hats going about their business of getting from one place to another, an almost zombie-like look on their faces. Such images added nothing of intrinsic value to his new virtual portfolio and so filled his electronic waste bin to overflowing.

Evidently he was missing something. He recalls going back to the dozen which represented the foundations upon which he was hoping to build, arranging those with people - Cath, Sophie, the Bakewell bridge - in a grid on his screen so that he could take them all in at once. He had been looking for a thread, something that linked them together; yes, they were all people, but there was something else about them, a common denominator, which made the photographs a success. After five minutes without lightning striking, he rose and went into the kitchen to prepare his dinner. Having left them on his screen, whenever he passed his desk he would jiggle his mouse to have them magically appear again, then stare at them for another minute or so before going off to do something else. Prepare dinner, repeat; put some washing on, repeat; hoover the bedroom and hall, repeat. It was only when he was sitting in front of the television a little over an hour later that it hit him.

He had channel-hopped and landed on the news. There was a piece about a rocket attack somewhere in the Middle East with footage of people variously running, screaming, shooting. It suddenly dawned on him that in those moments they weren't just people, they were individuals reacting to an external stimulus. The people from Trafalgar Square or outside Tate Britain were reacting to nothing; they were just going about the day-to-day. Was it any wonder that, from his perspective, they all looked dull. He nudged his screen back to life. All the people before him were reacting to an event, an external stimulus: the fixing of a lock and the throwing away of its key; enjoying the view of the river, and the joy of being able to do so completely naked; and Cath, reacting to the majesty of Siena - and before that, reacting to *him*. It wasn't people he needed to find at all; it was events where people were bound to be. As soon as they became absorbed in the external stimulus - magical or mysterious, murderous or marvellous - they came out of themselves and showed their true colours. That's where the honesty was, in portraits of people being forced to react to their surroundings.

Although he was unsure what he was going do with it, the revelation felt like a breakthrough.

✼

"How's it going, Neil?"

Just before the end of March, Rico rang him out of the blue.

"Fine, Rico, thanks."

"The new flat?"

"Just perfect. Working out really well. Thanks again for the intro to that agent."

"Feeling at home already? I'm glad." Rico paused just a second. "And work?"

"Dribs and drabs," Neil replied, "but increasing. Enough to get by."

"So you're not looking for a quick 'filler' job, then?"

Neil laughed and ignored the question.

"And I think I may have had a breakthrough in terms of my proper work."

"Ah, the infamous projects. That's great. And how's your love life?"

The question drew a spontaneous laugh from Neil.

As far as the former was concerned - the 'infamous projects' - Neil had given Rico a flavour of his ambition, partly because he felt he owed him an explanation, and partly because he wanted to give himself an excuse to turn down any offer of work. It would be a trial of his resolve if things started to get difficult financially, and he wanted to be as well-armed against his own capitulation as possible.

"Listen," Rico pushed on, "the real reason I rang you was to find out if you'll be in tomorrow. Around five."

"Five? I should be, why?"

"There's someone I'd like you to meet, that's all. A friend of mine. You might find them 'useful'."

Neil noted the way the last word was delivered in parentheses, as if it were substituting for another.

"Sounds intriguing. What else do I need to know?"

"Nothing. It should all become perfectly clear when you meet them."

They chatted a little longer, then Rico rang off with a slightly bizarre "Enjoy!", and Neil went into the kitchen to make a note on the calendar that he was due a mysterious visitor.

Breaking into his internal narrative for a moment to check his phone to make sure he hadn't missed a follow-up text from Beth, he still wonders if he had built-up any expectations between

Rico's call and the moment the doorbell rang at precisely five the following day. He remembers none.

One of the advantages of his first-floor flat was that the conversion, when originally carried out, had provided a discrete private entrance at the side of the building, its front door revealing a small lobby at the foot of a set of stairs leading up to what was effectively the hall proper. On opening the door Neil found himself confronted by a woman; silhouetted against the dusk, she appeared relatively tall and slim, a large handbag slung over one shoulder.

"Neil?" In spite of the question, she sounded confident and self-assured. Without waiting for a reply she held out a hand. "I'm Fliss."

Under the lobby light, Neil's confusion must have been evident.

"Rico didn't tell you did he?"

"Tell me?"

"My name?"

He shook his head.

"He didn't tell me anything."

"Ah." She registered the minor setback then looked over his shoulder at the stairs. "Well, can I at least come in and explain?"

"I told him I wasn't interested in taking any photos for him."

She laughed.

"Don't worry, this has nothing to do with taking photos."

He squeezed to one side to allow her to pass, her perfume - which he recognised but was unable to place - announcing her arrival. Closing the door, he followed her upstairs to where she had paused, waiting.

"Just to the right."

Walking to the centre of the lounge, she paused to take the room in, then dropped the bag from her shoulder and removed her coat, laying it beside her as she took a seat on the sofa. Neil felt her watching him as he moved to his single armchair; then he sat and offered her a smile. He guessed she was in her late twenties or early thirties, and his early impression of her physique seemed accurate enough. Perhaps a little too slim, nonetheless she fitted the mould of a woman who Rico would be happy to consider 'a friend'. She wore little make-up, merely sufficient to give definition to her cheekbones and enhance her lips which were, he thought, also a little on the thin side; yet in spite of that, there was something about her that was undeniably attractive. Had she appeared through the door of the riverside flat six months' earlier and presented herself as the subject of that day's shoot, he would not have been surprised. His three months of celibacy felt suddenly provocative.

"So," he said, attempting to regain an equilibrium he felt he had momentarily mislaid, "what can I do for you?"

She returned his smile.

"First, I think I need to clear-up a little misunderstanding."

✿

Rico rang Neil the following morning to find out how he had enjoyed his time with Fliss. It was difficult to describe what had transpired; to explain how, after no more than a quarter of an hour, they were both naked in his bed, he releasing weeks' of pent-up frustration. And then her calmness a few minutes later as she said "well, now that one's out of the way, let's see if we can't try something a little less frantic, shall we?". She had sounded like a consultant or a therapist, though her parting words as she pecked him on the cheek when she left a few minutes after six o'clock - "that was on the house" - were hardly those you would expect members of either profession to utter.

"She's a…"

"She's a businesswoman," Rico interjected quickly. "She's only doing what the rest of us do: try and make the greatest commercial gain possible from the talents she has. And she is 'talented'..?"

He left the question hanging, playfully.

"Oh yes," Neil replied, picking up the theme in spite of himself, "very 'professional'."

They both laughed.

"Good," said Rico, "I'm glad you think so. A little gift from me; one 'on the house', if you like. Just to say thank you for all your work last year."

"That's what she said."

"What?"

"'On the house'."

"Ah." Neil sensed Rico smiling as he spoke. "But it was my charity, not hers. Anyway, I thought it might do you good, a little physical release." His voice dropped into an octave of seriousness. "I know it can't have been easy."

"Should I say 'thank you'?" Neil asked.

"That is entirely up to you, of course…"

"Then - unconventional as it was - thank you. And if it doesn't sound too crass or crude or something, I needed that. Maybe I didn't realise how much."

"Do you have a pen handy?" Rico asked.

"A pen?"

"I'll give you her number. I've negotiated 'mates' rates' on your behalf. Just in case."

Bathing in the afternoon sunshine, there is a veneer across the scene as if the weather has coated it with a transparent layer of gold. Looking at the jigsaw of the city - and seeing people nearer at hand engaged in simple pleasures like walking or talking, playing ball games, or even, like him, just sitting - it is difficult to comprehend the panoply of things that actually go on under the skin of something seeming outwardly so benevolent. But Neil has intimate experience of the imperfections the varnish masks; the difficult, dark, painful, and seedy side of life. Fliss was just one atom in a morass of molecules; atoms jostling and bumping against each other, trying to find their place in scheme of things as he had been too. Perhaps as he still was, as everyone always is. It is a recognition which keeps him grounded, aware of his place, evidence as to how far he had fallen - and of how far he has subsequently risen, too. Was it also a city which encouraged segregation of the world into 'right' and 'wrong'? Was what he had done - photographing naked girls spreading themselves before him (and then subsequently enjoying a number of them carnally) - intrinsically 'wrong'? Was what Fliss had been engaged in - and was probably still engaged in - 'wrong' too? Or were they both simply examples of people rubbing along as best they could? The core difference as far as he could see - and the result of his unending analysis - was that Fliss' attitude to who she was and what she did was ruthlessly authentic, one-hundred percent honest. Unlike himself. Or the self before Bakewell; before the turning point at the beginning of that year.

He had called her a week later to establish the ground rules. After that they met once or twice a month, depending on how flush he was feeling, or on how much he needed the kind of release she offered. Their individual hours together - Fliss was very precise when it came to timekeeping! - became part of his routine, on one level as mundane as his trips to the supermarket. They served a purpose, kept him in balance, on an even keel.

They were food in a way, perhaps for the soul as well as the body, who could say? Until two years ago, when he decided he no longer needed her services (or could no longer guarantee his anonymity), Fliss had given him the ability *not* to think about something fundamental: women, sex, love. It had been liberating, a gift given at the right time and which freed him to concentrate on his work.

Having made the connection between events and people, he began to seek out the former. As a starting point he chose Hyde Park and its Sunday tradition at Speakers's Corner. It seemed a low-risk place to begin again: it was free, regular, and filled with potential - and a man with a camera would hardly look out of place given the number of tourists who paused to snapshot the theorists, the charlatans, the exponents of political bias, the religious, and the downright barmy.

That last weekend in March had shown the first promise of Spring and in consequence a reduction in the prevalence of heavy coats, hats and scarves. Neil strolled around the periphery of the amphitheatre snapping the performers and their audience. The most promising locations seemed to be behind the speakers, shooting into the onlookers head-on. He sought expression and gesture, conscious there was a great deal of finger pointing, laughter, and faces flushed and florid with anger. After about twenty minutes, he abandoned his pitch and wandered down through the park to the Serpentine where, from both the Knightsbridge-side of the lake and near the Princess Diana fountain, he took photographs of the hardy souls swimming at the lido. As he re-bagged his camera he made a note of the number of shots he had taken: eighty-seven. "Well that's something" he said to himself.

And it was. Back in Belsize Park he loaded the images onto his computer and began the ritual: review, discard, create a black-and-white copy of those with potential, review again, discard again. He paused between the cycles to make himself a coffee and a sandwich - a peanut butter and jam combo which had been recommended to him by Fliss as the ideal mid-afternoon sugar, fat and protein rush. After the second round of selection - and the sandwich! - he was left with nine contenders. That was how he viewed them, 'contenders'. He had decided nothing made it straight into the highest echelon, expanding the twelve into thirteen and beyond. First they would go into a kind of holding area or 'photographic purgatory' where they would mature, be interrogated over and over again in a 'last man standing' competition. Or last men. He had decided, in this new realm of his, to keep the bar high; relaxing the standard was the first step down the ladder - either that or an inadvertent slide down a snake of unknown length. From painful experience he knew you only discovered how far you had fallen when you stopped moving.

Eventually - perhaps after a week or so - he settled on three of the eighty-seven; which expanded the twelve to fifteen. Two of them had been portraits of the audience from Speakers' Corner: one, a man, head back laughing; the second, a woman apparently pointing directly at the camera (because he had been standing behind the speaker who had enraged her), her expression so furious that she looked more like an alien of human composition who was just about to explode. Taken on a long lens, the third was of a woman mid-dive between the banks of the lido and the Serpentine itself, something in her face and posture suggesting a combination of fear, excitement and anticipation in equal measure.

And so it began. Protests, sporting clashes, political rallies, celebrations, commemorations, exhibitions. Navigating his way across events at which people would be present - or occasionally through the lucky off-the-cuff capturing of intimate moments (the serendipity of photography!) - slowly the number of photos in his high-bar portfolio rose; simultaneously and unconnected, gradually the level of paid work also increased. By late Summer he had reached a pattern for the latter - between five and ten days per month - which allowed him to be confident he had enough money coming in to keep his finances in balance, and enough time to allow his 'projects' to move forward. The other aspects of his life, from the mundanity of supermarket shopping to his visits from Fliss, operated on a schedule that simply seemed to work. Looking back, he doesn't recognise it as spartan in any way, but rather efficiently ordered. There is an image in his mind of a life with the colour removed, as if doing so ensured a perfect fit with what he was trying to achieve photographically. In as much as it was liberating, it also seemed entirely appropriate in its lack of flamboyance; a philosophy he had constructed to pay for his past mistakes. Indeed, if it had been a kind of 'cold turkey', then it was brought into sharp relief on the anniversary of Cath's death when he forced himself to decide how to mark it, knowing whatever he did could set a precedent for years to come. In the end he simply stayed in his flat all day and did nothing.

Overall there was no real hardship in a life removed from the frivolous, paring existence back to its essentials. He rationed his seeing of Harry too, and for a few months saw him less than Fliss, the attraction of going out for a beer, socialising in public - even with his best friend - having lost much of its appeal. Harry had rung him often enough to check he was okay, at least in the first half of the year; but eventually he too accepted the new status quo and waited for Neil to initiate contact. Rico kept in touch from time to time too, until one day Neil realised he had disappeared into the ether, only starting to discover the part-truths of what had happened to him some time later.

It was a groove in which he ran up and down for four years, the first half of his thirties. More conscious of age now, Neil recalls feeling older than he actually was during that period. Perhaps it was the enforcement of discipline, the choice of exhibiting a degree of self-control and restraint normally associated with someone of more mature years. Perhaps a little like frivolity and colour, it was a time where age became irrelevant too. It had no influence on the catalogue he was building, none on his relationship with Fliss, and none on the commissions he was awarded nor how he carried them out. Half-way through that period he landed a small Condé Nast gig - his first for over five years - and, sent to Brighton to capture 'the flavour of a southern beach summer', was determined to knock it out of the park. And he did so in spades, finding a couple of images for his own portfolio which he kept to himself. Reunited with the magazine, he would work for them three or four times a year over the next two years - including two trips to Italy - strict management of his time preventing him becoming drawn into the travel-romance of his old life. He would allow nothing to compromise his hard-won balance, the degree of monotone by which he lived, the progress he felt he was making.

It was Beth who was to christen them 'The Wilderness Years'. But were they? It certainly wasn't how he had viewed them at the time, and looking back, scanning the past in the same way he allows his eyes to skip across the city below him, it still isn't. She had a point of course, and they have talked about that period often enough; but for Neil it was simply a time when he lived life to a different pattern, a different heartbeat.

Four

The call from Charles Watson had been totally unexpected. Indeed, it had taken Neil a few seconds to recognise the voice, locate the experience. The gallery. 'Europe: Modern Contexts'. The beginning of things.

"What are you up to Neil? You seemed to drop off the radar after all that Conde Nest stuff, but I heard from someone that you'd resurfaced, started working again. And as good as ever, by all accounts."

How could he possibly answer a question like that? There was a tale to be told, of course; little did he know it was one he would be articulating within two years.

"It's a long story, Charles". He tried to laugh it off. "But thanks for the encouraging words."

"Well, more than that hopefully. I actually rang to run something by you. We're having a general exhibition here soon - photography, of course - and I've a smallish space I still need to fill. When your name came up, well, it seemed to make sense to give you a shout. I still remember that dog in Siena! What do you think?"

The offer surprised him, not merely its coming out of the blue, but because it forced him to consider that others might have been taking a view on what he had been producing during the previous year. More than a view; a judgement of some kind.

"I'm flattered," he offered, "but I'm not sure if what I've been working on will be of any interest to you."

"As I say, it's a general exhibition, a broad church if you like. Why don't you send a few things over and let me take a look? No commitment on either side."

After dinner that evening, Neil sat at his monitor and flicked through candidate photos. Having only lived privately with his new collection, it was a strangely bizarre experience trying to view them as a third party might, someone other than himself, someone coming to them for the first time. No matter what he thought, the litmus test always came under just such circumstances. They could only be any good - 'worthy' - if others thought so too.

Charles had not been specific in terms of what he was looking for in terms of number or scale. Therefore, in order to offer him maximum flexibility, Neil decided he would send over nine images, each one cropped to a square, that way Charles could display as many or as few as he wanted in a grid, a line, a rectangle - assuming he chose any of them, of course. Making copies of what he felt were nine of his best - and those which would best fit a 1:1 format - he checked them once, fussed over them, checked them again, before finally emailing them. It was an activity which felt remarkably different even though the simple tapping of a 'send' icon to spirit his images into the ether was something he had been doing for years now. Locating that difference wasn't difficult: this was the first time in a long while that he had risked something that really mattered to him. Yes, the shots for his commissions, for Conde and the other magazines, were all important professionally - and financially! - but what he was now doing was important *personally*. It was his first attempt to validate his new work, his new philosophy. Even him. And what if Charles said 'no'? Only once or twice had magazines sent back things he rated but which they hadn't liked; in those instances it had been like water off a duck's back. Take it on the chin; move on. But this was another matter altogether.

He heard nothing for three days, then the call.

"Not what I was expecting at all." Charles' opening gambit sounded like the precursor to a rejection. For an instant Neil feared the worst, wondering how he would handle the fall-out. He needn't have worried. "Quite remarkable really."

"I'm sorry?"

"Your photos. Just great. We've chosen five of them; they should fill the space quite nicely. Do you want to come and have a look before we open; you know, give them the once over?"

Neil recalls declining the offer. To a certain extent it was an issue of trust. Beyond the hill, he imagines London's myriad buses going about their business. When you get on a bus you don't question the driver's competence, whether or not he can actually drive. You take it for granted, a given. He had seen Charles' work as a curator and exhibitor; he knew what he was doing. What could he possibly contribute by seeing the photos on the wall before the show? He smiles. That first show - "European Contexts" - had been entirely different. It had been his initial experience of public exposure; he had been excited, giddy. He remembers once it had opened how he stood against the wall that first morning and watched people looking. And when it came to exhibitions now, displaying the work of today's Neil, the Parliament-Hill-sitting Neil, it was different again. These days he demands much greater control over how his work is displayed; it is expected of him too. But then, in that window between then and now? Were there elements of relief and gratitude mixed in? Was he so thankful for the chance that, even if Charles were to cock it up, he felt it didn't actually matter? Or then again, had he regarded it as being of the utmost importance, the opportunity to get to another rung on the ladder? He likes to think he recognised that next rung could just as easily have been the head of a snake.

Subsequently he rationalised - and not without some help from Beth - that his apparent laissez faire had been because he knew he had to come to the displayed images cold. He had become so invested in them that they were almost a religion to him; they represented a belief system that was about to be put to the test. If that was the case, he knew he needed to approach them in as detached a manner as possible, to see them as everyone else would - the 'non-believers'. So he didn't want a preview, nor to have it reaffirmed by Charles that they were good or that they looked great on the wall. Such approbation, if misplaced, could have proven to be the worst thing possible! In a way he wanted nothing more to do with them - not until he walked into the gallery in the same way everyone else would, and to be greeted by them as if they were new and fresh and unknown.

Looking up at the sky he is reminded how people have a tendency to equate weather with emotions, the foreteller of favourable or unfavourable events. If you were the type to succumb to such fragile mumbo-jumbo, then today's bright sunshine would suggest that his meeting with Beth should be a joyous one; how could it possibly be otherwise on such a day? He checks his phone for a second text message from her, but there is none. Yet, even though he holds no truck with such superstitious twaddle, he recalls getting off the bus not far from the gallery, hoisting his collar against the rain, and fearing the worst. The photographs would be dreadful; no-one would see them; few would bother to come to the exhibition anyway.

At the entrance desk, grateful Charles wasn't there, he paid the nominal fee for an exhibition guide without mentioning who he was. He wanted to be a nobody. Ahead of him in the first room, the huge statement piece from 'the name' who was the big draw; it was the image they had used on the flyers, the tickets. A landscape, interpreted almost impressionistically; a blocky, heavily edited image. Neil didn't like it. It wasn't his thing, and - as he rationalised it later - said more about editing skills than those relating to photography. He had little time for keyboard jockeys; the computer whizz who took the average and used software and processing power to turn their run-of-the-mill snaps into something else. They were in an inferior league to him; he believed whatever he did with an image - like removing the colour or reframing or sharpening - never compromised the integrity of the original. Perhaps he hadn't realised his distaste for flagrant photographic dishonesty until that moment. Later Beth would tell him she thought his revulsion was a by-product of his new-found philosophy. Keeping his dislike in check, he dutifully strolled around the main room before heading into the second of the four being used for the show.

Based on what Charles had said, he expected to find his work tucked away in a nook or cranny in the last room, the sort of pitch given scant attention by patrons already wearied by photo-overload. But there, on the wall right in front of him, five of his images. They had been printed a little over half a metre square and arranged on the wall in the same way the dots are on the five-side of a dice. In the centre, the hands releasing the key, and surrounding it the Serpentine diving woman, the elderly couple in Bakewell, the furious listener from Speakers' Corner. And Cath, posing and smiling in the sunshine.

"They look rather good, don't you think?"

Neil was dragged from his reverie by Charles' voice, and turned to accept the offered hand.

"I thought you said you had 'a smallish space' to fill?"

"We did," Charles laughed, "but yours got promoted. I mean," he turned to face them, "how could we not?"

"Really?" Neil wanted someone to pinch him.

"Well there they are, right before your eyes!"

Neil looked back to the wall and noticed his name stencilled on the paintwork. His name, and no-one else's. His wall, and no-one else's. His photos, and no-one else's.

"I'm in shock," he said.

Charles laughed again.

"Well don't be. They deserve their slot."

The two of them strolled round the rest of the room together until Charles was called away, leaving Neil to explore the final two sections by himself. Before he left, he returned to stand in front of his own photographs once more, checking to make sure it was still his name on the wall. It was a mental pinching at least. Suddenly realising he hadn't properly thanked Charles for the opportunity - his faith! - as he left, Neil paused at the entrance, scanning back into the exhibition to see if he could locate him. When he failed to do so, he returned to the ticket desk. The young woman who had sold him his guide smiled up at him.

"Could you give Charles a message for me, please?"

"Of course."

"Just tell him 'thank you'."

She scribbled the two words on a piece of paper in front of her.

"And you are?"

"Neil. He'll know."

It was still raining outside. He felt like celebrating. Pulling his phone from his pocket, he knew his choices were limited to either Harry or Fliss.

❋

Had Charles' exhibition made a difference? Was that even a valid question? It so obviously did that it seems ridiculous he should still query it. Yet doing so is all part of this general cross-examination in which he finds himself engaged, as if it is vital he understands everything - not for the first time, but once again - to make sure he has all the details at his fingertips. He needs to decipher himself afresh before Beth arrives, to have held the mirror up close once more.

It would be true to say that he felt reinvigorated by the exhibition; at the very least it had validated his approach, proven that he was on the right lines and hadn't wasted the last year and a bit of his life. There *was* merit in what he was trying to achieve, even if he didn't truly understand it himself sometimes. Just beneath the surface he saw a triumph for honesty, simplicity, the black-and-whiteness of it all; and it seemed a victory for people over things. Yes, there had been a preponderance of landscape and nature in those four rooms, and perhaps that had helped his work to stand out; but he took to assuming his had been the only contribution to have been 'promoted' - Charles' word - and surely that stood for something. To use somewhat hackneyed phrases, he knew he would subsequently need to 'kick on', to 'take it up a level' - but in the immediate aftermath of the event he had no idea what that might entail. He scoured the 'Evening Standard' for upcoming events, opportunities for him to get in amongst the hoi polloi once more; he wondered if he needed to be more selective, to come up with a 'theme'. If it were even remotely possible that he could be exhibiting again at some point in the future, did he not need to show a more cohesive face to the world rather than the random shots just presented?

And then, a little less than a week later, Charles rang again.

"Come down from the cloud yet?" he asked playfully.

"I think so - though I'm currently working out what I should do next."

"Well, I may be able to help you there."

"How so?"

"You have an admirer."

"I have thousands of those!" Neil joked. Charles didn't bite.

"I daresay you've heard of Jimmy ____?"

"Who hasn't heard of Jimmy ____?! Legendary guitarist and rock band front man; good guy or bad guy, take your pick."

"Well, he was in the exhibition a couple of days ago and would like to speak to you."

"Me!" Neil felt winded. "Why on earth would Jimmy ____ want to speak to me? What have I done wrong?"

"Wrong? Absolutely nothing - well, not that I know of, of course…" It was Charles' turn to joke. "Apparently now that he's finally retired, Jimmy's writing his autobiography - or is having his autobiography written - and is looking for someone to photograph him as he is now. He's got millions of photographs covering his career, but he wants some current shots, including one for the book's cover, and - having seen your work in the exhibition - he has this crazy notion that you might be the man."

"I don't know what to say."

"Well, don't say anything. He says he's drawing up a shortlist and now you're on it. That's why he wants to talk. A kind of audition, I suppose."

"Who else is he looking at?"

"No idea. I asked him, but he wasn't saying."

There was a pause Neil felt disinclined to fill. He glanced around the room hoping - for the second time in a week - to locate someone who could pinch him. The flat was, of course, empty.

"So before you get too excited, from what I could gather it's nothing like a done deal," Charles filled the void, "but worth a chat. I took the liberty of suggesting you'd welcome the chance to talk to him. Was that okay?"

"More than okay, Charles."

"Good. I thought so. Which is why I also gave him your number and we agreed that, unless I rang him to tell him otherwise, he's going to call you tomorrow. Afternoon, probably."

❉

"You've said what you need, but not what you want."

Picking up the phone when it rang at one o-clock, even though the voice had been softer than he had expected, Neil still liked to think he had immediately recognised Jimmy's gravelly undertones. Then again perhaps that was just because he had been expecting the call. It hadn't begun well. When Jimmy thanked him for taking the call, Neil had said something sycophantic about "how could he not" or "it was his honour", a response that drew a disappointed grunt from the former rock front-man. He'd obviously heard all that before. Jimmy cut to the chase about the exhibition, saying how he'd been struck by Neil's photographs; Neil checked Charles had provided the relevant background. "The bones of it," had been the reply.

"Might you be interested?" Jimmy's tone was flat, non-committal. It sounded like he was going through the motions.

Neil recalls it now as one of those 'all in' moments, where you look down at the cards you hold and have to decide whether or not you think your hand is strong enough. Are there few such incidents in a single life that are truly pivotal? He glances to his right and where he had lain nearly eight years ago when Cath had approached him. That moment and how he responded to it, to her, had been a point of inflexion, an instant when his life had

161

pivoted. On a smaller scale, when he first succumbed to Rico had probably been another. And within the next hour?

Two years ago, Jimmy's question had opened before him like a baited trap, flashing in some garish neon, a combination of warning and enticement. And Neil had examined his cards again.

"It depends."

"How so?" Something in Jimmy's voice indicated the registering of an unexpected response, not the fawning 'yes please!' for which he had been prepared.

"You've said what you need, but not what you want."

"Explain."

"You *need* some shots, a portrait, a cover for your book. But if it was that simple, you wouldn't be talking to me; you could get any idiot with a camera-phone to take it."

"Have you met my wife?"

It had been a rhetorical question, a joke accompanied by a rattling laugh. A step forward; Jimmy engaged. And Neil did know his wife - not personally, of course, but from her days as a model, the magazine shoots, the tabloid stories. Some people said it was a miracle they were still together after everything they had been through.

"Not yet," Neil ventured to pick up the thread. The laugh from the other end of the virtual line echoed.

"'What I want'?" Jimmy then quoted back at him.

"I'm guessing you want the photo to be something more than an image of what you look like; I'm assuming you want it to say something else, something about you, about who you are, where you are, how you've lived. In a way you need it to encompass everything about you, everything that's in the book. It needs to be story in itself. You want a portrait not a photo."

Neil placed his cards on the table and waited to see if he had a good enough hand.

"Very clever, Neil," Jimmy used his name for the second time. "And how would you go about getting that?"

"I'd need to spend a little time with you. Maybe half a day. We'd do a short informal shoot first, just to get all the nonsense of introducing the camera out of the way, and then I'd just be with you for a couple of hours; drinking coffee, walking in your garden; you could talk to me about your career, your book; I could meet your wife; you and I could play snooker."

"You've seen those stupid photos of the house then?" The previous year's 'Hello' shoot - timed to coincide with the announcement of his retirement - had obviously been Rachel's initiative.

"I have." Neil paused, leaving it there. "And then after that we'd have a second, more formal shoot, once I'd got to know you a little better. I'm certain that's where the final image would come from because by then we should both have a better idea of what you want."

"You didn't need practice shots and conversations with the woman at Speaker's Corner."

The observation surprised him. It *had* been a good photo!

"She wasn't writing her autobiography," Neil offered. Jimmy laughed again.

"How much?"

"I'm sorry?"

"Apart from my time," Jimmy clarified, "what would you want? Money, I mean. Everyone has their price."

The comment sounded loaded, heavy with meaning; the kind of thing - Jimmy's weary experience of the world - which Neil would have to get into a photograph. *That* was precisely what he had meant.

"Honestly, I haven't thought about it," he replied.

"I don't believe you have," Jimmy said, sounding impressed. He mentioned a number.

It was more than Neil had earned in the last four months. His response - "that's fine" - came out in a semi-strangled way; he hoped he hadn't sounded needy or amateurish. There were a few seconds before Jimmy spoke again.

"What are you doing Sunday?"

❋

He was picked up at eleven by a uniformed chauffeur in a large white Jaguar, the two of them then purring out of London and into one of the leafier and more exclusive parts of Buckinghamshire. The gates to Jimmy and Rachel's estate (the only word he could use when describing it later!) swung open as the car approached, and they crunched down the drive towards a house that made the one he had photographed in Derbyshire look like a pre-fab. As the car pulled up, Jimmy and Rachel appeared through the front door and waited for him on the steps.

When the driver opened the door, Neil asked him to "pinch him". It was becoming a common theme.

"Sir?"

"Nothing; it's fine."

As the chauffeur moved to retrieve his things from the boot, Neil walked towards his hosts. Jimmy was slightly taller than he had imagined him to be, and - slightly taller again - Rachel, who - even pushing sixty-five - retained a certain poise and elegance that could surely be traced back to her modelling days. Jimmy looked more like a pensioner than a rock star, and within a few minutes had blown out of the water any preconceptions Neil may have been harbouring. His handshake was firm and sincere, his voice as soft as it had seemed on the phone; he had only briefly released Rachel's hand when they greeted Neil at the front door. As they walked into the house he was oddly expansive, leading them through a large drawing room and into what Jimmy called the conservatory, a single expanse as large as most other people's entire houses. Two sofas waited for them either side of an enormous oval coffee table adorned with tea things and a small plate of biscuits.

"I'll be mother, shall I?" Rachel said.

Neil wanted to be pinched again, but refrained from asking, certain that, in spite of his gentlemanly demeanour, Jimmy might not have hesitated. During a brief pause, what he had said to Jimmy over the phone about 'need' and 'want' came back to him, not as something to be repeated to his client, but to be asked of himself. How far had the exhibition and what he had done thus far taken him along either of those roads? And sitting there, hoping he was about to photograph one of the most famous popular musicians of the late twentieth and early twenty-first century, his own need and want would surely inform what happened next; not at this moment - the rest of the day was surely pretty much set - but in terms of what followed after.

"So," said Jimmy, pushing the plate of biscuits across the table in Neil's direction, "how's this going to work?"

The shock of being in control, of not being told by a legendary mega-star what was going to happen next, makes him shiver even now. He recalls how both Jimmy and Rachel were focussed on him, awaiting instruction; their assumption that he knew exactly what he was doing could have been powerful enough to make him wilt, turn him back into a child. Or a fawning fan. And perhaps he might have done. Even now, as he replays the scene, Neil is half-afraid that it will turn out differently; that his memory will betray him and he will find himself waking up somewhere else, a twenty-first century Bobby Ewing. What stopped that collapse? Perhaps the realisation that this was no interview; this was the real deal; he was 'the man'.

The chauffeur appearing with his camera bags and small portable spotlight, depositing them on the floor by his sofa, gave him his cue.

"We could have a few shots in here first, just to break the ice, and then maybe you could show me some of the house and gardens so that I can work out the best place for the proper session - though the light might not be good enough to do much outside today. And if we can just chat, you tell me about the book..."

"So that you can find out what I really want," Jimmy interjected. Neil smiled. "Then we'll play that game of snooker while Rach fixes us some lunch. We'll take the proper photos after that?"

"Perfect."

And it had been. After they had finished their tea, Neil pulled out his Canon and just snapped, telling Jimmy not to pose at all (that would come later). Soon he felt almost invisible as the couple leant into their sofa, discussing an upcoming charity event they were to be supporting. When he included Rachel in a shot it was obvious she knew, an old sixth sense kicking in, her chin slightly higher, her back a tad straighter. Thirty years ago she had been to die for. Hard man of rock or not, Jimmy hadn't stood a chance.

Having found some of the "Hello" shots on the internet, Neil was already moderately familiar with the house when they eventually walked through the downstairs rooms and out into the formal part of the garden. The library was impressive in a National

Trust kind of way; the music room even more so - but that purely in a Jimmy _____ way. In the library Neil asked about the autobiography - why now, what Jimmy expected it to say - and in the music room he asked about his career, the highs and lows, the songs of which he had been most proud. Rachel, who walked with them until they went out into the garden, chipped in with the odd comment, mainly anecdotes about her relationship with the band, her life with Jimmy. Never a journalist, Neil kept the questions friendly, palatable, using them as doors through which Jimmy could choose to walk - or not. And he didn't duck a single one. In the garden - "modelled on one in France, so I'm told" - they sat by a fountain and Jimmy reversed roles, asking Neil about his own career. He suspected he had been more economical with the truth than his host. As they headed back inside and toward the snooker room, Neil had paused on the flagstones at the entrance to the conservatory and looked back into the garden, its fountain, the immaculate borders. It was on a vastly smaller scale of course, but he suspected it had been modelled on Versailles - an observation he kept to himself.

After Jimmy had thrashed him at snooker - "too much time on my hands these days" - they had an informal lunch back in the conservatory.

"I think there's only one possible place," Neil had replied in answer to Jimmy's question about where he wanted to take the final photographs.

"The music room?" Rachel guessed.

Neil nodded.

"If you were a great novelist we'd use the library, a famous landscape gardener, outside; but you're Jimmy _____. You made music, and music made you. But don't worry; no cheesy shots with you holding a Stratocaster or anything like that. These are going to be portraits. In the end people may not even be able to tell where they were taken." There was a slight pause. "Is that okay?"

"Makes sense," Jimmy replied. "It's kind of what I was expecting."

Neil looked down for his camera bags but they were no longer there; Jimmy had already had them moved in anticipation.

If there is a residual fondness for the hour or so which followed, Neil feels it not for Jimmy - although his gratitude to him is undiminished - but rather for the process they went through. It wasn't just a question of posing his subject, lighting him, working out angles, the odd prop - and they did use one or two guitars! - but the mechanism of doing so. Was it all those hours spent in seedy riverside flats suddenly repaying him? Of course there was no need to tease and provoke the Great Man - he wasn't trying to sleep with him after all! - but some of the techniques he had learned about how to talk to a model, knowing which angles were good and those less so, the insight into how lighting affected the final image, all came flooding back. It felt like second nature; a rebirth almost. And if Jimmy had previously assumed that Neil knew what he was doing, then he would have been comforted by the control demonstrated over the whole episode.

There was a moment after about fifteen minutes when it seemed as if a switch was flicked. Jimmy started looking into the camera in a different way. Perhaps he had relaxed; perhaps he was suddenly at home in front of his photographer; perhaps he had realised what it was he wanted - and if so, also how he needed to communicate that through the lens into which he was staring. It is an instant Neil can recall as if it were yesterday; his reaction - "now we're getting somewhere" - was voiced internally. From elsewhere in the house music started playing; the band's greatest hits. Rachel's idea. Jimmy had smiled just a fraction when he heard it, and Neil clicked the shutter. That, he was certain, was one in the bag.

When he came to leave, Jimmy and Rachel stood with him on the main steps as they waited for Des to bring the car round. Neil was sure the shoot had been successful, and yet he was leaving feeling more like a family friend than a photographer.

"You know your business of course," Jimmy said, "but I'd like you to send me - what? - a dozen to look through; maybe a few more. And I want you to be absolutely clear about the *one* photo you think is the best; the one that should go on the cover."

"The one that says what you want to say?"

Jimmy smiled and Rachel stepped forward to give him a hug.

"It's been a blast, man," said Jimmy, offering his hand and dropping his guard for just a moment to provide an echo of the old performer. Neil could only take it as a compliment. "I didn't think I'd enjoy it, but hey, what do I know?"

They laughed.

Jimmy's payment was in his bank the next day, the first of three days during which Neil slipped into his trusted cycle of duplicating, editing, refining; making them all black-and-white. From the shots he had taken in the conservatory, he ended up selecting three: one each of Jimmy and Rachel individually, one of them talking, tea cups in hand. It was so domestic, so normal, he wasn't sure if Jimmy would be interested in it, but he wanted to give him the option. Apart from two shots taken on a whim when they had walked round the house - in one, Jimmy pointing to a painting on the wall as he explained how he had been introduced to the artist - the rest came from the music room. There were only two with Jimmy holding a guitar - in spite of Neil's promise about not using a Stratocaster (and it was actually a Gibson Les Paul) - the rest either full-face or upper-half portraits, the majority with Jimmy looking directly into the lens;

in the remainder he was glancing off to the side. The photo taken just as the music came on was an absolute peach. The smile on Jimmy's face was only hinted at in the merest upturn at the sides of his mouth, a glint in his eye; it was a photo all about memory. Yet though a stand-out, for Neil it was not the cover shot. That was the second photo he had taken just at that magic moment fifteen minutes in, Jimmy staring so completely though the lens, his eyes incredibly clear; it was a picture which simply said 'this is me, now'. It was the face of someone who had lived, whose life was etched in every line and blemish such that you could inspect each of them and trace it back to a specific time, the event that put it there. He had sharpened the image just a little and when he eventually sent them all through he named it 'this-is-the-one'.

And it was. When the book came out two months later, that was the Jimmy who stared back at his readers, the photo that said 'this is me, and this is what you're going to get'; it was a portrait that spoke to both the past and the present - and cocked a snook at the future. Just like a rock star is supposed to. Jimmy almost smiling became the very last page in the book, and for the other inserts Jimmy chose the one of Rachel, the one with the painting, and one of the ones with the Gibson.

On publication day he sent Neil a case of champagne and a copy of the book inscribed simply "Thanks, man. Jimmy".

For the next two weeks or so Neil couldn't escape Jimmy's face; it started out at him - Jimmy's face, *his* photograph - from the window displays of bookshops and underground escalator posters. And the man himself was doing the rounds on television chat shows. Neil likes to think the Jimmy the public saw on those occasions was a man inhabiting the mask expected of him; he didn't seem too much like the guy he had photographed. But whether the real man or the rock star, lots of people knew Jimmy; the tentacles of celebrity were wide-reaching, a web woven by the celebrities themselves and their agents. Neil has come to wonder if self-promotion isn't a type of perpetual motion, a never-ending vortex feeding off itself; and he has concluded that the one single thing such people have in common is the potential to sell themselves, who they are and how they look, something unique which belongs to them alone.

Should he have been surprised when he was contacted by an ex-England footballer finding himself in the same boat as Jimmy: autobiography coming out, needing a photo or two with which to adorn it? Or the doyen of the stage who, in preparing for her one-woman show - "the last thing I might ever do!" - needed some artwork for flyers and the posters which would decorate the exterior of Wyndham's Theatre? As much as he had struggled to draw a line between her and Jimmy - how many degrees of separation were there?! - Neil hadn't believed her 'last thing' comment at the time, a judgement later proven correct by a recent triumph as Mrs Bennett in a Jane Austen-inspired mini-series for internet TV. Not having posed the question as to what the exact consequence of his shoot with Jimmy might be, it was with naïve surprise he found himself inserted into that same celebrity web. He had made Jimmy look good - some said great - and there were plenty of people who wanted a slice of that particular action.

Over the next three months his diary gradually filled. After the footballer and the doyen, there came a steady stream of people wanting to have him work his black-and-white magic on them: a TV gameshow host, a retired politician, two more sports stars, a singer - and desperate ex-Reality Show participants trying to stop the spotlight going out. He was very clear with everyone: no colour, total honesty. He trotted out his 'what-you-need-versus-what-you-want' line where appropriate. Most of the reality show contestants faded away into the background; they needed colour and soft focus, the fabrication not the truth. Was it ironic, given how they had stumbled into 'fame' via a 'reality' show, reality was the very thing they were trying to get away from? The

National Theatre called and asked if he would consider a retainer to come in from time-to-time and provide them with images from their dress rehearsals which they could use as PR. He specified the same rules about black-and-white and honesty, and they accepted - their actors loved it too. How could they not?

"It's been crazy." He had been sitting with Harry in a Hampstead bar, the two of them catching up on the four months since they had last seen each other. Neil's debrief was inevitably by far the longer.

"Did you really have a shoot with Petra ____?" Harry had always had a soft spot for the ex-soap actress.

"As part of the NT thing, yes." He paused. "And since then one or two others where you'd wet yourself if I told you about them."

"Who?!"

Neil smiled.

"I can't say; not yet. Sorry."

"Bastard!"

They laughed.

"And I bet it pays well?" Harry changed tack.

"Just a bit better than location shoots and those homes' magazines." Neil left it understated knowing Harry would think of a number and then double it. Would he be close? Neil doubted it.

"You'll soon be a celebrity yourself, Old Fruit, if you keep going on at this rate. You'll need someone to take *your* photo!"

"Oh, I think I could manage the odd selfie!"

He had intended to tell Harry the news about Fliss but didn't seem able to find the right moment to insert her into the conversation. Would Harry have cared anyway? Historically he had been sceptical about Neil's involvement with her, and in the early days of their association counselled him against the relationship. "It's an arrangement, not a relationship" Neil had protested. "Yes, of course it is - and I'm the Pope!" had been Harry's rejoinder. But now it was an ex-arrangement, an ex-relationship.

If Neil had begun to be concerned about Fliss, how she might fit in with this new life that was accelerating away with him, he was spared the difficulty of raising the topic because she beat him to the draw. They had been in his flat two weeks previously, he - as ever - conscious of the time, knowing she would soon be leaving, when she propped herself up on her elbow and stared at him.

"I think we should call it a day, don't you Lovely? Now you're making your way in the world again, becoming public property, the last thing you need is to have a link to a person of dubious moral character."

"You're one of the most honest people I know," he replied.

"Maybe - but I'm not talking about honesty."

They had debated his situation - and Fliss made it clear that it was *his* situation - but it was no more than going through the motions; she had made up her mind, the course was set.

"But I'd like you to do me a favour," she said, once he had accepted her premise and its conclusion.

"Anything."

"Take my photograph. Not for show or anything like that; and not for me either. But for you, to remember me by."

So Fliss stayed beyond the allotted hour in order to allow Neil to photograph her, and as he did so he realised that on this occasion what was needed and wanted had everything to do with him and nothing at all to do with her. How did he want to remember her, that was the question? When he had finished and put his camera away, they had sex one more time, a bizarre way to say goodbye.

As she stood on the threshold of his flat, about to take her first step out of his life, she smiled and said "that one was on the house".

She was as right about him becoming 'public property' as she had been about most things over the two years or so he had known her. He was invited to be interviewed on the radio - a five-minute slot on Radio 1 or something more in-depth for Radio 4 - and declined. "This isn't about me," he had protested. It had sounded feeble, probably because it was. Then day-time TV approached him; would he consider an appearance on a breakfast show, or one of those late morning chat shows? He declined again.

And all the while, after each shoot, after each commission, he would trawl through the photos he had taken and add some of them to his virtual portfolio. Often the ones he chose were not those he submitted to his clients; inevitably there were some that spoke more to him, said something about the shoot, the day. He kept one with Jimmy and Rachel drinking tea on the sofa, for example. Going through the process, keeping an eye on that high bar of his, was the professional thing to do. He hoped it also kept him grounded; he could always go back to the original dozen and measure anything new against them. Did they stack up? Did they meet his undocumented criteria? Was he making sure that his integrity hadn't slipped?

Not only professional, it was prudent too, and when Charles rang - just over a year after the call about Jimmy which had launched him on his crazy journey - Neil was prepared.

Five

Her voice. The memory of the first time he heard it in person hits him so hard, is so tangible, that Neil looks round from the bench on which he sits to check she hasn't crept up on him. Although the people he can see are all different now - a steady stream of players, walkers, picnickers, lovers - in a way everything appears exactly the same as it did when he first sat down around an hour ago. Even though her voice is there, Beth is not. Not yet. Prompted, he glances down to where his phone rests in his lap, sees her latest message just as it arrives.

NIGHTMARE! JUST PARKED UP NEAR YOUR HOUSE. WILL BE THERE IN ABOUT FIFTEEN MINUTES. DON'T MOVE!

Fifteen minutes in which to try and reach a conclusion; fifteen minutes to complete his story, a reflection triggered by the impending meeting, the echo of her voice, the way it had triggered Cath's "Do you often take photographs like that?" which was the sentence that opened the floodgates to his life. Fifteen minutes? Probably nearer twenty.

"You must be Neil," she had said blowing the walls of the gallery asunder.

Charles had been at his brilliant best. Once Neil had chosen the images he wanted to exhibit, Charles took on the role of administrator, contacting the photos' subjects where he could to ensure they were happy their face was included in the exhibition. The vast majority were already in the public domain so there was no issue with those, but some were not, kept back in his private collection. These additional few seemed so fundamental - both to what he was trying to achieve as a photographer as well as in portraying the 'sitters' themselves - that he wanted to show them, to give as rounded a display as possible. One or two objected, but most people were fine; when Jimmy saw the shot Neil wanted to use of him and Rachel taking tea he just laughed and told Charles that Neil was "a sentimental bastard".

He had taken a hands-on role this time in terms of how the photos were printed and where they were hung; it was a solo show after all. He had decided that his statement piece, the one visitors would see first, staring at them as they crossed the threshold, would be the one of Jimmy almost smiling. Given what it represented, where it sat on his journey, Neil felt it deserved pride of place. Part of him would still have loved to have had it for the cover of Jimmy's autobiography, but its layers of meaning only became evident once you had met the man - which therefore made it perfect for the end of the book. But now? He had chosen it for the simple reason he thought it the best he had taken that day.

He and Charles had debated how to arrange the images, and settled on two options: chronology and theme. They could either be displayed in the rough sequence in which Neil had taken them - a proposition supported by having Jimmy's face front and centre - or by genre: musicians, sports stars, theatricals etc. Although Charles favoured the latter, mainly because he argued doing so would make them more immediately accessible to the audience, they eventually chose the former. Neil had argued that, if the images were hung by theme people might decide to only see those in which they were interested - sporting icons but not politicians, thespians not TV personalities - and in any event, this exhibition was as much about his journey as anything else, so shouldn't they do their best to give people an opportunity to experience that too?

A little detached from those shuffling in front of him along the walls, he had been standing alone near shots of an NT cast rehearsing "A Midsummer Night's Dream" when, having approached him unseen from the side, she had spoken.

Dressed in a sharp dark navy suit - tailored jacket, pencil skirt - over a white blouse accented by a small but vibrant brooch, he knew her instantly. Hers was a face which regularly accompanied features for the BBC, their London Arts correspondent.

"I'm Beth Chaplin." She extended her hand.

"Yes," Neil said, taking then releasing it, "I know."

"Oh dear." She laughed.

"Why 'oh dear'?"

"It would be nice to be a little more anonymous sometimes. When people realise who I am, it can put them on their guard."

"Really?" He smiled. "Well I'm completely defenceless."

She laughed.

"Work or relaxation?" he asked; then, when she frowned, clarified. "You being here, I mean."

"Ah." There was a brief moment as she considered her response, glancing away from him to the photographs and then back. "The latter - probably."

"Only probably? That sounds a little duplicitous."

"Well, if it turns out to be just me looking at your wonderful photos, then it's relaxation and that's fine."

"Which sounds as if there's another reason; a work-related alternative."

She looked away again. Neil examined the shape of her head, the cut of her hair; wondered how she was able to create such a wonderfully melodious voice, so rich and soft. Unique. Well, almost.

"Tell me," she said, turning back to him, "the photo of Jimmy and Rachel; was that posed?"

He laughed in spite of himself. A couple of people turned and glanced his way.

"Not at all. That's how they were; just a middle-aged couple taking tea in their slightly less-than-modest conservatory."

"It may be my favourite," she confessed.

He inclined his head; raised an eyebrow.

"Because?"

"If what you say is true, it's so completely genuine."

"Then I'm guilty as charged."

When she started to walk slowly away, she made it perfectly plain that he was expected to accompany her.

"I've spoken to some of my colleagues in Radio," she delivered the phrase as if it were one she could throw away, of no consequence whatsoever. "They said you'd turned down an interview - twice."

"Does that make be a bad person?"

She smiled.

"Not bad - but interesting. I think there's a story to tell - Bakewell and all - about how you've suddenly arrived, what you did before. A human story. And you're interesting too because most people would relish the chance for their 'fifteen minutes of fame'."

"Is that all it is, 'fifteen minutes of fame'?"

"For some people, yes." She stopped walking, pausing near a photograph of an ex-world champion Formula 1 driver. "But in your case, I'm not so sure."

"In my case?" He laughed again. "I don't think I've ever been 'a case'."

When she said nothing he found himself filling the void.

"All I do is take photos of the real stars. I'm just an anonymous guy. It's not like I'm Don McCullin or anything! People know his name; they don't know me from Adam."

"Of course you're not McCullin. You're you; and you're right, people don't know who you are - not yet. But you're the man who took these fantastic photographs; you're the link between normal people" - here she gently waved a hand towards those meandering through the gallery, eyes focussed on the walls - "and some of their heroes. You've seen them, spoken to them, interpreted them and their lives through your camera; that elevates you above anonymity. Whether you like it or not." The final phrase was delivered with an edge; she said it as if it were a fact, undeniable and incontrovertible. It told him not to argue. "And all of that means that you are - as the police might say - 'a person of interest'."

Captivated, he laughed once more.

"This time *not* guilty, Your Honour. I was miles away when the crime was committed!"

"If I might," she said, smiling, "I think the evidence" - another wave of a hand towards the walls - "demonstrates we can locate you *exactly* at the scene of the crime."

They had almost reached the end of the exhibition and had come to a halt in front of a small number of non-celebrity images, ones that Charles had persuaded Neil to segregate because they didn't quite 'fit'. He stared at the Bakewell bridge lovers.

"That's really where all this started." He said.

She followed his gaze.

"In Bakewell?"

He nodded.

"That's some journey, Neil."

"Well, the second half of it, anyway."

He stared at the key, those few inches between it and the fingers releasing it, the gap between them charged with magic, and hope, and perhaps - in the end - loss. Who could say?

"Would you tell me the story? All of it?" She asked the question without looking at him, for a moment unable to take her eyes from the photo in front of them.

✿

What was he supposed to have said, approached like that, by her? He told her he'd think about it, and she gave him her card and asked he call her once he had made up his mind. Sooner or later he would have to talk to someone, she argued; sooner or later *his* story would become public property, as much as Jimmy's and the rest were. And hadn't he already made his contribution to ensuring that happened, that all their myths were perpetuated? Would it not be dishonest to refuse to submit himself to the same scrutiny?

He rationalised that if he agreed to an interview with Beth there was a chance he might maintain a modicum of control over the story; surely better that than to have some amateur piece together fragments stolen from all over the place and concoct a damaging fiction. Worse than that, a dishonest fiction. He thought of Rico and of Fliss. And he thought of Cath, and how negatively her narrative might be played out. He also told himself that once his own was out in the open - authorised, from his own lips - then that would be it, he would never need to be looking over his shoulder, never have to worry about turning the pages of the Evening Standard in fear of coming across some cock-and-bull depiction of his life. It might also give him the chance to close a door that had remained ajar for far too long. He had seen Beth's work. There had been a piece on the Summer Exhibition at the Royal Academy he had found insightful, sensitive. She had covered exhibitions elsewhere, interviews with theatre and film stars at openings and premières; though unsuccessful, she had been nominated for a national journalism award. There could be no doubt that she was a serious person, good at what she did.

There could also be no doubt that she was an attractive woman just a few years younger than him. Did that play a part in his decision-making? Sitting on Parliament Hill looking down into the city where they had first met, he likes to kid himself that it did not - but what subsequently happened, and her impending presence alongside him, is evidence to the contrary. But perhaps most of all it was her voice that seduced him; its promise and its echoes. If he were to sit and talk about his life, then surely he would derive some pleasure from doing so with someone who spoke as she did.

He checks his watch.

He had called her the next day; told her that, subject to agreeing the format - and the boundaries - of the conversation, he was inclined to accede to her request. He would give her a précis off-the-record to allow her to build some structure, outline some questions, and they would go from there. What she had in mind was what she called a 'cosy chat', the two of them facing each other, comfy chairs, relatively subdued lighting. There would be minimal crew present, probably just a cameraman and a sound engineer, and afterwards they could sit through the recording together, agree what if anything would need to be cut. At that point, she told him, she'd have a view whether to recommend it for TV or radio. Both were possible.

"I have an idea about the former; I might be able to swing something. Of course, if it turns out to be rubbish then we'll not use it, and it will turn out to have just been a cosy chat after all."

In that moment he felt as lost as when Cath had said "Do you often take photographs like that?". It was recognition that made him shiver then as it does now. And what made his reaction the most significant was that he had spent the last four years insulating himself, reestablishing control. His black-and-white life. And there he had been, suddenly submitting himself to a woman with the voice of an angel and who liked to wear vividly-coloured jewellery.

※

"How did I start? How does anyone start anything? Luck? In my case it was an old Zenith 35mm; a Christmas present in my mid-teens. It seemed exciting, exotic, grown-up even. I think I'd used up the first roll of film within the day, but then came the waiting; that long drag before you found out what you'd captured."

"It was frustrating?"

"Intensely so. But maybe it feels more extreme looking back from where we are now. Digital technology gives us answers in an instant - and lets us play with them too. Immediately."

"But all that waiting, it didn't put you off?"

"I got used to it. After a while it seemed I always had a film or two at Boots or Max Spielmann's, one in the Zenith, one or two ready and waiting to be used. Sometimes, when you got the prints back, you'd be surprised with what you'd taken; more than once I found myself thinking "I don't remember that!". If they were any good, then that was a doubly happy accident."

"But you were hooked?"

"Completely. Don't ask me when it happened, or if there was a moment or a photo that did it, but it was a path I was soon heading along. And when I got my first digital, well, that was it really. From that moment I never wanted to do anything other than be a photographer."

"But you could have been, couldn't you? You were a bright enough student, you got decent grades at school. If you'd wanted to, you could have pushed yourself harder, chosen a subject to study."

"Ah, but I *had* chosen a subject, it just happened to be one that was less conventional, not 'taught' per se. Not then so much. And I didn't see myself as an academic either. I carried on to do 'A' levels because I could see that some level of qualification would be needed to get a job - and I was smart enough to know that I needed a job to eat, to live."

"So you never had any doubts?"

"About what I wanted to do, or whether I would be successful?"

"Both."

"None about the first; always about the second! I knew - I *thought* I knew - that I was okay as a photographer. I mean, some of my early shots were good, and I used to look at others' and think I could have done better, or would have taken them differently. I could find fault with composition or exposure. All that gave me a confidence, I suppose - though I could have been completely wrong, sadly misguided."

"Yet wouldn't it be fair to say that it was luck rather than talent that got you your first break?"

"As with most things, it depends on your point of view... Look, this is difficult... In a way it starts with Cath. I met her because I was taking photographs, because I wanted to be a photographer. Is that luck? I happened to be on Parliament Hill - my favourite place in the whole world - taking photos and she happened to be there and saw me and walked over to talk to me. Luck? Or fate? Or something else? Was that encounter destined to happen the day, years before, when I unwrapped my old Zenith?... I'm not a philosopher, so I can't answer that one. But luck?... I suppose so - not that luck's ever enough, not on its own. But it happened, it was lucky - for me, that is. Not only did I know what I wanted to do with my life, but I seemed to have found the person I wanted to spend it with."

"She shared your passion?"

"At first I thought she might. I mean she seemed interested. But in the end, not really, no. Her ambitions - for her, for us - were much more conventional; you know, house, family. That was where she was most strongly rooted, I suppose. Her upbringing had been different to my own: I couldn't wait to get out from home, she struggled to leave hers."

"But she did?"

"Yes, she did."

"What was the trigger that allowed her to take that step? As you say, your sights were set on something else, a different vision of the future."

"I don't know... I mean, I loved her, and I guess she loved me too, well enough... We went to Siena and I took my first real photograph - "

"The one known colloquially as 'The Pissing Dog'?"

"Yes. That was lucky too, of course. But it gave me even more confidence, and I came to the conclusion that I might be able to engineer a future to satisfy both ambitions, hers and mine. Perhaps in a way it made me even more determined to succeed at being a photographer - whatever the cost."

"Whatever the cost?"

"I guess I didn't see it like that then. Maybe it's a view I've inserted subsequently, as if proven by events... But then? I thought that if I made it as a photographer, then why shouldn't we have a house, a family? I didn't see them as incompatible at the time."

"And are they?"

"Incompatible?"

"Yes. I mean, how do you think about that today?"

"Hmm. The jury's out on that one..."

"Okay... Ralph, Cath's father, played a major role in your progression, didn't he?"

"I'd like to think that part wasn't so much luck - though it was undoubtedly my good fortune that Cath's father happened to be loaded - and well-connected. I showed him my work, he liked it, pulled a few strings. Soon enough I had a small slot in the 'European Contexts' exhibition Charles Watson had put together, and after that a few commissions - work for Condé Nast. I kidded myself that I was beginning to build a modest reputation; after all, I thought my photos had begun to speak for me - though I know now I had nothing really to 'say' back then. It wasn't that *they* were lucky; people liked them because they were good."

"Tell me about Rico. He was not the sort of person one would normally choose to be associated with."

"I didn't know that at the time... Look, I was green, and when he approached me - all smooth and sophisticated with offers of better paid work - I suppose I was swept off my feet. For the second time. It seemed as if Rico - who I'm not ashamed to say I've actually always liked - was giving me the chance to keep both those dreams, both those balls in the air."

"But you found you had to drop one of them..."

"Not really. I actually dropped it without realising I'd done so... I was stupid. The calendar stuff was semi-innocent, easy enough to excuse away. But the glamour work that followed... I closed my eyes to what I was actually doing, seduced by the notion that there I was, 'a professional photographer', thinking that allowed anything, made everything acceptable."

"But you were seduced by more than just being the guy with the camera weren't you?"

"I can't remember how it happened - or I don't want to - but soon it was more than just about taking photos with some of the girls. It was difficult... Or maybe it was too easy. And I really liked the girls. But that's no excuse. I was weak, that's the bottom line. I was taking photographs, earning money; I told myself I was still working on both dreams, that we would be able to save enough, that I could get out when I wanted, give Cath what *she* wanted... But I was being massively dishonest; first to myself, and then to Cath."

"She knew what was going on?"

"I told myself she couldn't have. I mean, she seemed so disinterested in what I was doing, my photography. She was gradually becoming withdrawn - which only succeeded in making the girls more attractive. I say it that way round, but it probably wasn't, was it? So I think she did know, and I think she was trying to insulate herself against it. Maybe she was hoping I'd come to my senses... But it ruined her and corrupted her dream, just as I was corrupting myself I suppose. Inevitably I missed it. I was so wrapped up in what I was doing, living this 'life' I'd created for myself, a kind of self-indulgent sex-drugs-and-rock-and-roll lifestyle - though without the drugs and very little rock-and-roll - that I missed her slide away from me; I missed her decline. She had tried to get me to change, to stop; she had, in her own way, cried out for help. Even Ralph had seen it and found he had to stoop to ask me to intervene, but I was too self-absorbed, too blind…"

"You were surprised then, when she committed suicide?"

"'Surprised' is such an inadequate word… In that one moment it felt as if I'd been hollowed out, left empty. As if someone had held up a mirror and I was looking at myself - the real me - for the first time in a long while. And it was too late. When I went back to the flat, traces of her were everywhere, and yet I knew she was never coming back. There had been a moment - there are always such moments, some good, many not so - from which there is never, ever, any going back. Maybe I learned then that you can't retrace your steps. Learned it then, but only saw it a few months later."

"And then came Bakewell. Did that learning start then? Tell me about Bakewell."

"Bakewell? I think it might have been my friend Harry's idea. Not Bakewell itself, but getting away. It was almost Christmas, just a few weeks later, and I'd been stuck in the flat pathologically embarked on my own decline. Perhaps it was mourning or grief, I don't know. How can you know what things are when you experience them for the first time? Anyway, something made me decide to get out, away. It was just happenstance that I ended up in Bakewell at Abi and Clive's marvellous little hotel, with Clive's wonderful food. Being there forced me to pull myself together a little; you know, clean myself up, dress a little better - less time in my pyjamas! It forced me to talk to people - just a few - and it made me go out, walk about, start looking outwards again."

"And you took some photographs."

"I'd only picked up my camera once since the day Cath died, but on Christmas Eve I took it with me, walked around the town a little bit, took some shots."

"How did that feel?"

"I don't know. Strange at first, I suppose. I was self-conscious, that's for sure. An odd sensation; ironic, considering. But maybe once I'd started…"

"And in the end they weren't just any old photographs you took, were they? The ones of the locks on the bridge, the people there; one or two of those are quite special. Iconic, even. I know one in particular garnered a great deal of praise at your recent exhibition."

"Yes. Thanks… At the time you're never quite sure - in terms of how good a photo might be. It's not like there was a long delay like there used to be with the old Zenith, but I still had to wait until I got back to the flat, downloaded them into my software, could examine them properly."

"But you knew then?"

"I guess so. Especially the ones with the key, the hands. They seemed to be about so much more than what you could simply see. I think that's important in a picture, don't you?"

"And that's when things turned around for you, is it? Because the world didn't hear much from you - one way or another - from just before that Christmas for - what? - a couple of years. Were they really wilderness years?"

"That's an interesting phrase. You might say the year before, when I had been working for Rico, you might say *that* was the real wilderness time… But, yes, there were - gradually - bits and pieces of me that emerged; like that shoot I did of the house-and-home thing in Derbyshire some months later. That was the first time I'd come out of my shell, I suppose. But I know what you mean."

"So Bakewell wasn't some kind of epiphany then?"

"Not at all, Beth. What was it? The break in the middle of a slide, perhaps. Or another period of mirror-looking. I think it did save me though; I mean my camera and those photos saved me. They gave me something back, something I'd lost; they gave me something to aim for. Not that I could really articulate it then - and maybe I can't even now - but they set me on a path, if that doesn't sound too hippy."

"You drew a line?"

"I sorted out the flat and then moved out of it completely. It wasn't expunging Cath from my life, nor trying to rid myself of guilt or anything like that; at least I don't think so. After all, how can you erase your past? But if I was going to survive - however melodramatic that might sound - I had to give myself a chance, a fresh start. And professionally, if you like, the Bakewell photos did that. They were the foundations, the touchstone. There was something about them that told me what I could do - or what I should do."

"How so, Neil?"

"Oh, form and content I guess. At a simple level, anyway. Black-and-white, for example. I realised how much closer black-and-white got you to the heart of things. Stripping away colour, distraction. In the hospital - where Cath died - I had sat in a corridor outside her room, waiting... There had been some photos of staff on the wall; large black-and-white prints of nurses, doctors, pharmacy staff, porters. All smiling, looking friendly, helpful, professional. But most of all you could see that they were genuine; people who were there to help, on your side. Those photos - that sense of honesty - haunted me. Maybe it still does. But it provided something that informed my choices."

"Choices? About your photographs?"

"Partly, yes. Not just that I should focus on monochrome - in an attempt to get at 'the truth' if you like - but that the real stories were in people, not in landscapes or buildings. And in people just being themselves, not laying on a bed with their legs spread pretending to be something they weren't. Or trying to get the viewer to fantasise about being someone they weren't, or to imagine things that were - I don't know - dishonest. Because that's what it came down to. Away from the photos, I mean. That notion of honesty versus the dishonesty of my past, if you like. I wanted to try and capture the honesty of people in simple black-and-white - just like those hospital corridor shots. Maybe I thought that would redeem me somehow. And I tried to live a simple black-and-white kind of life too, You know, be honest with myself, without compromise."

"Yet you took commissions for other things - after a while I mean. Like the Derbyshire house you mentioned. Hardly black-and-white, and not a person in sight!"

"You're right, Beth. But I had to live, to earn some money. I found I was able to distinguish between work and what I felt - no, *knew* - was important to me."

"Rico offered you work didn't he? A return to what you'd done before. Were you tempted?"

"I don't know. I'd like to think not - at least not too much. It would have been easy, of course, and I could have done it. It would have ticked boxes; short-term financial ones, for example."

"And perhaps others? The girls?"

"Indeed… But I knew if I went back to that old life then I'd never get out. I would be condemning myself, giving up. And I thought I deserved one more shot. That my photos deserved one more shot. That sounds pompous I know, but how else can I explain it?"

"So you pursued this 'black-and-white' lifestyle, but it wasn't sterile was it?"

"In what sense?"

"Professionally? Emotionally?"

"Emotionally? That probably depends on your point of view... The commercial work I did, that was fairly sterile I suppose. It was a job I went about as professionally as I could, and the results were obviously okay; I mean, there was repeat business. Even Condé Nast gave me work again. But I invested as much of *myself* as I could in what I thought was important, in building up a portfolio based - quite simply - on people; people in situations, reacting to things. That's where you can draw a line all the way back to Bakewell... Everything else I kept as routine and functional as possible, investing as little of me in it as possible."

"Everything?"

"Pretty much."

"And then, out of the blue (as it were!), Charles Watson calls you."

"We talked about luck earlier on, didn't we? If you were planning to ask me if that was lucky, then I don't know. He called me because I was visible again - out of your 'wilderness' perhaps! - and because my photos were good. At least the ones he remembered. He wanted to see what I was up to, so I sent him a few shots; Bakewell, some other things like the screaming woman in Hyde Park. He liked them and found me a slot in a show he was putting together. For the second time. I owe a great deal to Charles, of course. I fear there are a lot of people like him - probably in all sorts of professions - who don't get the credit they deserve, working away more or less in the background, making things tick, helping people get better."

"Like your nurses in the hospital corridor?"

"I hadn't made that connection, but if you like, yes."

"And as a result of Charles' show and the prominence he gave you in it, you had a call."

"Indeed. Of course you can say it was lucky that Jimmy ____ happened to visit Charles' exhibition, but lucky that he rang me? My photos did that. That's what he responded to. He didn't know me from Adam, but he liked what he saw, and on that basis thought I might be able to give him what he needed. Which it seems I did."

"How was that, photographing a legend?"

"Honestly? It was wonderful. I loved every minute of it. And the thing I liked most - about Jimmy, I mean - was that he was entirely genuine. I'd been nervous that he'd be some old rock god who was so far up his own image of himself that he'd be a bore, impossible to photograph. I was worried that he'd be a fake, I suppose. But not a bit of it. It was a great day and, I have to say, I think we both got out of it what we wanted."

"Well it certainly started the ball rolling."

"Jimmy has lots of friends and connections - and obviously lots of people read his book! The phone hasn't stopped ringing since. It got me a raft of work photographing some wonderful people. I've been very fortunate I suppose. And then Charles - for the third time! - with the recent show... That seemed to go down really well. I think people liked that. And all that's got me here, talking to you. Does it get any better?! Is that luck? Maybe that's one you can answer for me!"

"Perhaps... But why *are* you here, Neil? You've turned down interviews before, I know."

"I have, you're right... A number of reasons I suppose - not least is that I met you in person, and I knew of your work... But it occurred to me that sooner or later, like it or not, I'd have to tell my story to someone, and now seemed as good a time as any, before it got out of hand."

"Meaning?"

"Oh, you know; people making stuff up with the result that you spend all your time denying things that didn't happen rather than being truthful about what did... I still don't really regard myself as 'newsworthy' in any case. In my own mind I'm still just the anonymous guy behind the camera."

✧

It didn't occur to Neil until later how alien it had felt to be on the other side of the camera. Nearly two years further on, he is used to it a little more, having come to terms with what he calls his 'minor celebrity', caught in the reflected glow of others' stardom. Very occasionally it feels a little like shrapnel, ricochets from those times when he has photographed the less-than-perfect. Mud sticks. But back then? As he, Beth and Will, the director, had been editing the interview - the visual as well as the audio - the notion of him as subject gained traction. It had, he thought, been a good session, and from what he could see there was little which needed to be cut; perhaps the odd sentence here and there, the odd question. When he was asked to approve the final edit he did so in the privacy of his flat, Will having sent him a file for him to review on his computer. If he hadn't been totally aware of what he was looking for at the time - still wrapped up in the novelty of it all - he knows now.

As another means of preparing himself for today, he had replayed the interview once more the previous evening. The oblivious city stretching below him, he sees it in his mind again, remembering their conversation more for what was *not* in there. They had spoken a little about Cath - fulfilling the request he made to Beth in advance of the session - and not at all about Harry, material that most likely would have been cut in the interest of time: Will had found an ideal broadcast slot for the piece, but there were constraints.

Some three weeks later the interview was aired on a BBC2 arts programme, the second feature in a line-up of three. If the interview had been slightly surreal, watching himself on television proved even more so. Harry had come over to the flat to sit through it with him, his response to Neil's request for some 'moral support.'

"You're a natural," Harry had said as the show's presenter moved onto their third package, "and that Beth's a real looker. You're clearly second best on that front!"

"Thank God for that!" he had said.

Not expecting any more messages from her now that she has liberated herself from her car, he checks his phone anyway, then glances over his shoulder to examine the figures walking across the heath, into and out of his view. He knows she will crest the rise in one of two places depending on the route she chooses to take from where she has parked. He also knows that watching for the moment when she will hove into view would be a futile activity.

She had rung him the day after the programme aired. She said she'd like to know what he thought of it in the cold light of day; and she'd like to thank him for the opportunity. Could she buy him dinner? There was a place she knew not far from Portland Square; it was usually fairly quiet after seven-thirty.

"There's one thing we didn't really talk about."

That had been her opening gambit. They had dispensed with the general chit-chat, and covered the interview at the most superficial level: his impression of it, how he thought he came across, the ambiance of the set, how the piece sat within the overall programme.

"What's that?" Neil asked, sensing they were getting closer to the real reason they were there. The starter having been pleasant enough, it felt as if Beth was serving up the main course.

"The time after Cath's death, up until now..."

"The 'Wilderness Years'? What about them?"

"You were very specific about not wanting to talk about - how shall I put it? - the 'emotional side' of that period."

"Because there was very little to talk about." He tried to see if a straight bat would work, all the while wondering why she wanted to know; after all, the interview was over and they were hardly likely to re-shoot it based on any new evidence coming to light.

"But there was not nothing," she suggested.

"Why not?"

She laughed.

"No-one has a period of two years of nothingness - even when they're completely wrapped up in their work, as you were."

"Why are you interested?"

It was a question he simultaneously asked himself: why *was* she interested? What difference could it make?

"Because of you. Because in spite of all your black-and-whiteness, I can't see you as a sterile, unemotional, unsatisfied hermit. It simply doesn't fit." She fingered her wine glass before raising it from the table. "And because my intuition tells me that there's something there."

"That you need to know?"

"Need? No, not really. But want, most certainly. A loose end I'd like to tie up. Just for me."

She uttered the last phrase as if it were a favour, and Neil thought about his habitual need-versus-want question. Sitting on Parliament Hill, he recognises it now as a question he was actually applying to himself at the time *about* her.

"Not professionally? Not as an interviewer? Not to end up as a note in a little black book ready to be trotted out at some point in the future?"

"I don't," she said, her face darkening a shade, her voice - suddenly wrapping itself about him and lashing him to her will - taking on a more serious tone, "have a 'little black book'." She was on the verge of being offended. "That's not the way I work." A slight pause. "I'm asking more as a friend than the person who interviewed you. There's a gap I'd like to fill. For myself, not the BBC."

He watched the wine glass travel to her lips. Had there been the merest trace of a tremor? For a moment he held her eyes, suddenly surprised how deep they were; and there was a slight flush on her cheek. The wine perhaps, or a trick of the light.

"I did see someone, occasionally. You're right. But it was never going to be long-term."

"Nothing serious?"

"I wouldn't say that." Neil wondered if, in it's own way, the relationship he'd had with Fliss had been the *most* serious of his life. "But it always going to be temporary, time-bound."

"Friends with benefits?" she suggested, attempting to be playful but not quite carrying it off.

"Possibly. Or possibly not in that order... It was an arrangement that suited us both for a while."

Beth raised her left eyebrow at the phrase and placed her glass back on the table.

"Sounds almost calculated."

Turning to his own wine, Neil let the remark go. There was only one further step to take, but he had gone far enough already.

Even if he didn't understand it, his sense of loyalty to Fliss was strong, one he did not wish to betray.

"And now? Where is she now?"

"I don't know; I've not seen her for some time. And am unlikely to." By the way he spoke, the raising of his own glass, he hoped to suggest the topic was closed, to give Beth the message that was all she was going to get.

A brief silence descended. Message received and understood.

"You do know what happened to Rico don't you?"

The juxtaposition of the two topics threw him instantly. Had she known there was a link between he and Fliss all along, or had she simply changed tack, unaware of the thread that bound them together?

"I can see from you reaction that you probably don't."

"I haven't seen or heard from him in quite a while either," Neil said, trying to restore a modicum of equilibrium.

"Ah... Well you won't, I'm afraid. A few months ago he was arrested and went to trial. He was convicted just before our interview. I assumed you knew."

"Convicted?"

"His legitimate interests - like the magazines you worked on - proved just a front for a raft of less 'wholesome' activities. Drugs and prostitution, mainly. He was essentially a small time crook the police tolerated because they had bigger fish to fry; but eventually there were just too many indiscretions for them to ignore." When Neil said nothing, she continued. "Sorry, I thought you knew. Hence my remark in the interview."

It took Neil no time at all to not be surprised, after all didn't that explain perfectly the shoots, the girls, Fliss?

"But I liked Rico," he said, as if responding to another challenge or speaking of the dead. Or justifying his own actions. "He was never anything other than straight with me. And - believe it or not - caring and generous." He saw the look on Beth's face. "Oh I'm sure that's surprising. Yes, he was smooth and slimy in many ways; a showman, an 'operator'. But he never took advantage of me."

Beth went to speak but changed her mind, waiting a moment before she asked him about upcoming commissions, who he would be photographing next. It was a clumsy Segway into something else, and although they carried on talking and eating for another thirty minutes, the evening was suddenly lost.

"I'm sorry," she said. They were standing outside the restaurant, about to go their separate ways. She placed her hand on his arm and left it there. "I didn't mean to...you know."

"It's alright." Neil looked down at her hand. "I guess I was a little bit thrown. I hadn't expected the questions - or your news."

"Will you give me a second chance?"

"Of course." He smiled. Although he was unsure what sort of second chance she needed, how could he refuse her? If there had been anything unresolved between them - perhaps the unanswered from the interview, the unknown about his past - it was surely a boil that had been lanced. He could envisage her giving him no more pain. Her grip on his arm tightened a little as she leant up to kiss his cheek.

"Thanks. I'll call you."

In spite of the apparent tenderness of that farewell and the words she had spoken, Neil could only interpret it as Beth saying goodbye. Even now, as he recalls her walking away from him, he somehow remains convinced - against all subsequent evidence to the contrary - that it was the last he would see of her. And why was that? Not simply because what had started out to be such a promising evening had pirouetted before nose-diving into disappointment, but also as a consequence of the cause of that collapse. Even though he had not been dishonest, he couldn't help but interpret the scene - from Beth's perspective - as his seeming so; the topic about which they had pivoted, and the way he had so evidently shielded Fliss, could only be viewed as cover-up rather than discretion. This would be doubly true if Beth had either done her homework or had managed to put two and two together - a theory endorsed by the way she had turned the conversation from his period of supposed emotional sterility to Rico. If she had indeed arrived at 'four' as the answer to a 'two-plus-two' equation, then how could she not walk out of his life?

Had that prospect perturbed him? He certainly stewed on it for the next day, asking himself how he really felt if she had indeed been saying goodbye. And then there was the corollary to that; further self-interrogation as to why he was asking such a question in the first place! It had been a cat-and-mouse game of second guessing, and one in which he could only be the loser.

He cannot recall whether he had actually reached a conclusion - on any of it - when she rang him two days later. Had there been surprise in his own when, on recognising that voice of hers, he actually spoke? Knowing it was impossible not to give something away, he hoped not. Making no reference to their dinner, Beth said she had rung to ask him a favour. To Neil it felt as if she was drawing a line, though under what he was unable to articulate; nor was he able to identify what lay on the line's other side.

She was going to a photography exhibition in a couple of days and, in spite of it being unlikely to be "his kind of thing", wondered if he would mind accompanying her. There were two reasons for the request, she said. The first was to benefit from his professional expertise. The second was that, knowing the photographer concerned would be there (she mentioned a name that failed to resonate), she didn't want to be hassled by him; she wanted to avoid any attempt on his part to curry favour based on the assumption she was going to review the show - which she was, of course. Neil's being at her side would offer her some kind of protection, discourage interference, perhaps even to the extent of giving the impression that she was there on her own time. Although disinclined to accept the first premise, Neil accepted the second at face value and, knowing he could be free on the day in question, agreed to her request. The analysis - of both her asking and his accepting - started almost as soon as the call had ended and rumbled on without conclusion until the moment when, standing waiting on the pavement outside The South Bank, he saw her walking towards him from the direction of Waterloo Bridge. Given his frequent assignments at the National Theatre, that part of the river was all too familiar to him; less so was the sensation that he felt on seeing her, at its heart the relief that their damp squib of an evening meal had not been the last time their paths would cross.

She had been right about the exhibition. The photographer had taken mundane, everyday objects - a saucepan, a child's teddy, a magazine - and placed them half-hidden within a landscape, the supposed premise being a comment on the intrusion of the material and commercial on the natural world. It was the kind of fabrication Neil disliked. Having semi-disguised the offending articles in each scene, for most exhibition-goers it was a visit which soon descended into a puerile version of "Where's Wally?", each image a puzzle to be solved rather than a photograph to be looked it. The landscapes themselves not only played second fiddle but eventually became almost invisible. Even Beth succumbed once or twice, grabbing his arm with a plea for him to "Look at this!" or "Bet you can't find the potato peeler!". He made a show of trying, but he wasn't concerned in the least whether he would succeed or not. However, what *did* soon matter to him was that he was there with her. It was the first time he had been anywhere with anyone for a very long time. For obvious reasons he and Fliss were never seen outside the confines of his flat; and for similarly obvious though very different reasons, Harry - with whom he did socialise - simply didn't count. He felt a vaguely familiar warmth he could not immediately place, a sense of attachment that disturbed him, and when he looked at her as she stood a little way away from him, trying to find a dustpan and brush in a formal garden, he imagined an invisible cord striving to join him to her. It was a sensation for which he could find no words, but it was one to which he grudgingly found himself acquiescing, as if he had been given a gift at Christmas he had yet to realise he both wanted *and* needed.

"I suppose you get used it it," he said once they were outside, pausing on the walkway overlooking the river. There had been no plan beyond attendance at the show.

"Used to what?" she asked.

"People staring. I noticed it a few times, people looking your way. They must have recognised you from the TV; it was that kind of a look. Do you get that often?"

She smiled.

"On and off, yes. Sometimes it's actually quite nice, sometimes not. What's most embarrassing is when they come up to you and ask for your autograph, and then - to make matters worse - realise they've nothing on them suitable for you to scribble on!"

He laughed.

"What do you do when that happens?"

"I've taken to carrying a few Post-its in my bag, just in case. Not because I want them to have my autograph you understand - I mean, really! - but just to get them out of the way." She paused.

"And anyway, you shouldn't assume they were just looking at me."

"How so?"

"Oh, once or twice I saw people looking *your* way. You forget, you've been on the telly now. And with me, to compound the error! Someone, somewhere will have watched our interview, and where are you most likely to find those kind of people if not at a photography exhibition?!"

Whether it was the look on his face - one of realisation, shock, or horror - that made her laugh he couldn't say, but laugh she did. And as what she had said dawned on him, the ridiculous nature of it, he couldn't help but laugh too. It was a combination that turned the heads of a few passers-by.

"What now?" she had said once they had settled down, glancing across to the heart of the city as if the answer was buried there somewhere - like a spoon in a forest! - and all they had to do was to go and find it.

He couldn't help but look that way too; Charing Cross, Victoria Embankment, Somerset House, then The Strand and into the depths of a largely hidden but inexhaustible city.

Her hand finding his own roused him from his reverie, his celebration of the city he loved.

"Second chance?" she asked. She was smiling.

✾

Looking over the city, Neil visualises the journey they took that afternoon, retracing their steps as they walked towards Charing Cross Bridge, Beth releasing his hand as they ascended its steps after which they remained unlinked for the rest of the journey. Traversing the river, they continued alongside the station, and then up toward the South African High Commission and Trafalgar Square. It was clear Beth had a destination in mind, and Neil had been happy to allow her to set the direction. He recalls a slight moment of panic when they traversed Charing Cross Road, concerned that she was heading for the National Gallery. He had never mentioned Cath's affinity for the place, nor realised how the prospect of visiting it again - and with someone else! - might potentially affect him; but at the last minute she steered to the right and aimed for the Portrait Gallery instead. He remembers the slight rising inflexion in her wonderful voice as she turned the word "tea" into a question, then continued on without hesitation as if his response had been both affirmative and immediate. He had said nothing.

The annual exhibition for the BP Portrait Award was on and, rather than head straight for the café, she diverted them into that, and they meandered about the rooms much as they had done an hour or so earlier. He remembers his attention being split between the portraits, Beth, and watching other people. After their conversation outside the South Bank, he was partially preoccupied in trying to catch people looking at *them* - and then, if they did, to see if he could define whether they were looking at her or him. However, they seemed more anonymous there, and he caught no-one eyeing them with anything approaching obvious recognition. As far as looking at Beth was concerned, how could he not? It hadn't been to fulfil any analysis of her physical presence - how she looked, what she was wearing - but a rather more metaphysical one; what was she actually doing there, and with him?

Knowing she will be with him soon, he looks down at his watch, the sun glinting from its surface, and remembers glancing at his hand in the gallery as if the imprint of her fingers might still be there. What had her hand-holding been about, given it had been so temporary? Was it simply to secure him somehow until she was confident he was attached and would follow her across the bridge, the river, and beyond? And if so, how far? Or was it something else? Unbidden, Camden Market comes to mind and the occasion Cath first took his hand. She had not let it go for the rest of it day. Neil wonders if that represents a parallel or a contrast, uncertain if it is the first time he has created such a comparison.

At one point she had called him to where she was standing, asking him to admire a portrait that was so realistic it might easily have been a photograph.

"I don't like it," he said.

"Why not?"

"If you wanted a portrait that looked a photograph, why not take a photograph?"

"But you have to admire the skill."

"Yes, of course. But isn't it the job of the artist to interpret what they see in front of them? In a way, *not* to paint exactly what's before them? If all they do is replicate, then what's the point?"

Bereft of either the skill or the inclination to aim for the ultra-realist, most of the artists did interpret of course, a few taking their interpretation so far that the end result hardly resembled their sitter at all. Neil remembers the debate - ultra-realistic painting versus photography - as a vague thread accompanying them as they walked around the gallery, and one that joined them for coffee and cake later.

"Is this better?" she asked as they sat drinking, terminating a brief lull that had been filled with the general café hubbub of conversations and clinking cutlery.

"Better?"

"Than our dinner and my ham-fisted attempts at conversation then?"

"Hardly ham-fisted, but better, yes," he smiled, resisting the urge to reach across the table, half-expecting her hand to make the journey itself.

It did not. And in not doing so, he was assailed again by questions as to her motivation, her presence - those then expanding to begin to ask the same of himself. It would have been easy for him to have declined her invitation, to walk away when they emerged from the South Bank exhibition; he could have made an excuse, fabricated some small lie to extricate himself. And yet he did not.

Their first kiss - their first proper kiss - answered a number of those questions only to replace them with others. But it was not one to be shared that afternoon. As they were about to leave the café, their next destination undefined, Beth's phone rang and a brief conversation ensued. It transpired that a Grand Dame of the theatre had just died and the BBC needed all suitably knowledgeable correspondents to try and get quotes and interviews as soon as they could to enable the corporation to include something meaningful in that evening's news bulletin. Neil had photographed the lady concerned and offered Beth his view in two short sentences which she duly noted in a small pad rescued from her bag. He promised to send her some images when he got back to the flat. Now recalling her seamless transition into journalist-mode with a smile, it had seemed as if someone had flicked a switch, Beth morphing into a second version of herself, the professional woman. Outside, as the taxi he had flagged down for her pulled to the kerb, she kissed him briefly and was then gone, lost in the throb of the city. Later, what struck him most about Beth's departure wasn't the suddenness of it, but the way it demonstrated the two sides of her personality. More than that, it was proof - if proof were needed - that the Beth with whom he had walked through the portrait gallery was the private one.

"You realise." he said, watching her as she returned from the en suite, his dressing gown wrapped loosely about her shoulders, "that I know next to nothing about you."

"Oh." Beth slipped out of the robe and placed it across a nearby chair already laden with her clothes. Neil watched her as she moved, the flexing of the muscles in her arms, shoulders, thighs; on one level she astonished him, though as yet he had been unable to give that astonishment a name or to attach specific attributes to it. Other than her voice. "And is that such a terrible thing?"

She slid into the warm space she had left behind and shivered slightly, encouraging Neil to wrap his arms about her once more.

"Not terrible, no. Just a little - imbalanced."

"How so?"

"Well you interviewed me; you know all about me, my whole story."

"Your 'whole story'?" She echoed the phrase playfully. "I doubt that very much. But if what I know is all there is, I might as well get my coat." She made a show of pulling back the covers as if she was going to get out of bed again, forcing Neil to pin her back against the pillows. He stopped her laugh with a brief kiss.

"You know what I mean."

She wriggled from his grip and sat up slightly, propping herself on an elbow to look at him from an even height. It was a pose which prompted a flashback: Fliss in almost exactly the same place, the same position, telling him that this would be the last time he would see her. And now here he was again, Beth's body almost a mirror-image, though with vastly different expectations to Fliss' last visit.

The Sunday after the National Portrait Gallery they had met near Marble Arch. The location had been Beth's idea; she told him she wanted to see where he had taken the photographs of the two women, the one diving and the one screaming. Coming from the tube, as he waited at the lights to cross Cumberland Gate he saw her leaning against the railing near the entrance to the park and Speakers' Corner. She was casually dressed - baggy tracksuit-type bottoms, trainers, sweatshirt beneath a loose woollen wrap-around top - and carrying a soft shoulder bag decorated with an abstract floral pattern. It was the uniform of someone very clearly 'off duty'. Catching sight of him when he was half-way across the road, she eased herself away from the fence and walked to meet him, her greeting - a soft kiss on one cheek placed perilously close to his mouth - seemed a logical follow-on to how they had parted on Charing Cross Road. She slipped an arm through his and told him to "lead on".

It was strange retracing his steps from those many months earlier - and doing so without his camera and with a woman on his arm. Not exactly an interrogation, initially it felt as if his replaying that day were a test of some kind, not of memory but of application, a form of justification. That it was nothing of the sort made little difference. Neil knew Beth was interested, trying to understand what happened, how he had come to capture those particular images, two of which had proven to be so pivotal for him. As they wandered briefly between the speakers, occasionally pausing to listen, he couldn't help but wonder if this were an extension of her interview, as if she were dotting 'i's and crossing 't's. Or was it Beth's attempt to close a chapter - or open another one? After fifteen minutes they drifted away, following the paths he had taken that day, across the park and down to the lake. Eventually they paused on the bridge where he had taken his first shots of the swimmers, and then strolled along the southern edge of the Serpentine towards Rotten Row and then on to the park entrance near Apsley House. They slowed and came to a natural stop near the small takeaway café; once again they had arrived at a point where - from his perspective at least - their next move was unplanned.

"Coffee?" His question had been the obvious one.

Beth looked at the café and shook her head. "Not here."

"Knightsbridge? Piccadilly?"

"Would it be alright if you showed me where you live?"

As he laughed, she pulled him towards her, head angled back slightly, inviting him to kiss her - which he did, gently at first, then wrapping his arms tightly about her, with more urgency. For a few seconds he felt fused to her, as if their tongues had become one, their breath as one. When he opened his eyes he expected to be somewhere else - coming out of a dream, perhaps? - but the sound of the traffic returned to him as did her request. She laughed and squeezed his arm, leading them toward Hyde Park Corner tube station, in charge once again.

They took the Victoria line to Leicester Square where they changed, waiting 5 minutes on an increasingly busy platform for the Northern line train to take them to Belsize Park. When it arrived they were forced to stand, pressed together, their conversation only sporadic against the rattle and roar of the tunnels. At one point as the train rocked, Beth's free hand found Neil's waist in order to steady herself; she left it here for the rest of the journey until she took his hand on leaving the train.

"Do you ever take the stairs?" They were waiting for the lift to carry them up to Haverstock Hill.

"All 136 of them? Sometimes; but only when it's much busier than this."

Ten minutes later Neil was leading her up the stairs of his own flat and, in spite knowing how organised and tidy he was, found himself desperately trying to remember what sort of state he had left it in. They paused in the lounge, his vague and open-ended "Well…" acting as a break.

"Why don't you put the kettle on and then give me the tour?" Beth suggested. "But first, point me in the direction of the bathroom."

When he emerged from the kitchen - the kettle switched on, the cafétière and two mugs prepared - he expected to find her waiting for him in the lounge but the room was empty. He walked into the hall and saw the bathroom door was open. After a short panic brought on by the sudden notion that she might have had a change of heart and fled the scene - a panic measured in terms of the few feet between bathroom and bedroom - he found her standing near the foot of his bed scanning the room, her woollen wrap deposited on a chair.

"Decided to start without me?" he asked.

She walked toward him and placed a hand on his chest.

"As if."

Her undoing of a button on his shirt was all the sign Neil needed. He pulled her to him and they kissed again, this time fervently at first, then more softly. She broke away from him a little to undo the rest of his shirt buttons; he found her flesh beneath the bottom of her sweatshirt, then grabbed its hem. She raised her arms to allow him to pull it over her head.

"Wow," he said, softly, involuntarily, surprised by her shape, how she was just a little more voluptuous than she had appeared up to that point. Surprised by that, and stunned she should be there at all.

"My turn," she said, returning her attention to his shirt, freeing it from the waistband of his trousers, slipping it from his shoulders.

As Neil loosened his belt and Beth stepped from her tracksuit bottoms, he realised she had already removed her trainers, leaving him to fumble with his shoes. She waited until he was freed from his trousers then moved close to kiss him again, pressing herself against him, her lower abdomen against his growing erection. Moments later they were lying on the bed.

It had been months since Fliss had been there and he was suddenly aware of his pent-up frustration. Having been taken aback afresh by how beautiful Beth was, he wanted her instantly, to engulf her. But that was how he had begun with Fliss, and Beth was not Fliss; this was a different situation entirely. As much as anything else, Fliss had been a teacher, and Neil remembered the things she liked, the things she told him to do; and so he desperately tried to ignore himself and to focus on Beth, to explore her as slowly as he could, to savour the moment, to use his fingers and tongue, the magic of touch. He tried to pretend that this wasn't their first time, that he wasn't as desperate as he knew he was; he tried to be as selfless and considerate as he could be, dedicating himself to as much of her as he possibly could, until the moment when - with her almost at climax - he could contain himself no longer, and lifted himself up, guided his penis inside her, and then, pushing harder, rhythmically, released.

She held him there, lying on top of her, until he was completely diminished, then she let him to roll away, freeing herself to slip out of the bed and into the en-suite. He had just about regained his breath when she re-emerged, returned to the bed, shivered, allowing him to wrap her in his arms again. Then came his statement resulting in Beth raising herself on one elbow, looking into his eyes, her left breast resting on his upper arm.

"The Beth is short for Bethany, not Elizabeth - in case you were wondering. I'm thirty-three years old; thirty-four in a few weeks. I studied Journalism and Art History at university after which I moved to London to work for the BCC, which is where I've been ever since. I've lived in Newington, Haringey and Muswell Hill, but to be honest never really liked any of them very much. I have a mild allergy to cats, and my favourite place in the world is - bizarrely - Belgium."

"Must be the beer," Neil suggested.

"Can there be any other reason?" She laughed. "There; you have it in a nutshell."

"And men?"

"Three locked in my cellar. All the dead ones are buried at my old place in Haringey - but don't tell anyone."

Neil wrapped his arm around her again, pulling her a little closer, his free hand combing through her hair.

"You know what I mean."

"The skeletons in my cupboard? We all have them, don't we? Mine? I married far too early and divorced far too late. Chaplin is my own name; always has been." She paused, running her fingers across his chest. "I think scars are important, don't you? They're the things that teach us how to live; what works and what doesn't. Mine have made me wary of men who have none, who profess love based on an untested and unadulterated notion of what love is. Alarm bell rings when I see a man who has not been hurt hard."

"Because they'll end up hurting you all over again?"

She laughed softly.

"Quite the opposite. I'll probably end-up hurting them and be the cause of their first scar, and I don't want that kind of responsibility. Or guilt."

"Doesn't that - I don't know - 'narrow the field'?"

"Interesting choice of phrase…" Beth took her time to consider the premise. "Probably. And it makes me more cautious too; more self-protective, I suppose."

"So I qualify because I have scars too?"

She looked at him unflinchingly for a moment, then raised herself up to kiss him gently on the lips.

"You? Oh, *you* qualify in all sorts of ways," she laughed again, "except when it comes to making coffee!"

✿

He had then made coffee of course. He thinks about the rest of that day, how they had eased through it, gently navigating their way through what was a beginning - though of what he had been unable to say. From the edge of his peripheral vision something red catches his eye, and he watches as a Frisbee floats through the air. The way it is being chased confirms it is wildly off-course, though the squeals of laughter from children behind him suggest its deviation may not be entirely the result of chance or incompetence. As a man retrieves it from the grass, Neil thinks about that first day with Beth and about chance, how it came about and what it then led to. Or is still leading to. The biggest question of all.

How soon it became evident that Beth fitted him like a glove he is unable to say. They slipped into a new routine effortlessly, both clearly delineating between professional and private lives, neither intruding much on the other. When they were together they were indefatigably together, on private time; they discovered shared loves and pet hates, and when these diverged as they inevitably did sometimes, they found themselves able to adjust, compensate, make allowances. Neil wondered how much the absence of pressure from Beth came down to her past and the way she lived with her wounds, because there was no pressure, not for a very long time. The phrase she had used during their interview - "friends with benefits" - has come back to him more than once, and does so again as he sits and looks, interrogates the landscape, and waits.

He recalls searching for evidence of her self-professed scars during those early weeks and months; recalls the search and coming up empty-handed. With respect to her marriage, she never told him how early "too early" was, not that it seemed to matter; it was sufficiently distant for her to have made her peace with it and for the trauma left behind to heal, at least on the outside. It was something she never referenced again and of which he saw no tangible evidence. If you were to meet her for the first time, to enjoy her company as a new friend, you would never have guessed that she had experienced such anguish. Perhaps it had been the making of her in a way, investing in her a kind of independence and self-reliance that was, undeniably, part of her allure. When Neil tries to put together the jigsaw of the Beth he has come to know, her independence is perhaps one of the cornerstone pieces. There are others too, of course; her intelligence and wit, her voice and beauty, and perhaps her general competence at being a decent human being. Having identified those early on and placed them in their appropriate locations, she is a puzzle he feels he is now a little closer to completing.

But what of himself? As he came to understand more of her, clicking those pieces into place, when did he realise that the puzzle was in fact double-sided with him on the verso face? And what was it that Beth was likely to be seeing? During those first months together - now stretched all the way back nearly two years - was she too going through the same process of sifting, filtering and composition?

He spoke little of Cath - and not at all of Fliss. She remained a spectre of which Beth would surely have an inkling, a ghostly presence hovering benignly in the background. If Beth regarded Neil's experience with Cath as a scar of equivalence to her own, she never said. The difference, from Neil's perspective at least, was that he remained profoundly *un*reconciled to it in spite of the reboot it had triggered, the part it played in shaping how he had subsequently started re-living his life, inventing a new philosophy, his photography, everything. A direct line could be drawn from Cath to Fliss, and now he had sketched a another leg on that particular map. In a way he had embraced his pain, chosen to confront and challenge it, not squirrel it away in a darkened corner. Had his approach really been that different to Beth's? There were times when he wanted to compare notes with her, to surface "the truth, the whole truth, and nothing but the truth" as if doing so would offer them both something cathartic. It seemed, suddenly, as he checked his watch once more, his phone, glanced over his shoulder, that it could be a condition on which they might move forward - if that's what they were going to do. And taking that path would require his coming clean about Fliss, reconciling them both to her role in his journey. It was the kind of knowledge that could make or break.

In that instant the metaphor of puzzle-solving was displaced by the entirely more appropriate notion of a photograph developing. When Cath had died not only did he discard his old life and the majority of his old photographs, but he set about processing a new image. It was the idea of the black-and-white life. He had nurtured it, built a vision of what it should look like, how it should be composed; he had been diligent, taken care to ensure nothing extraneous had slipped into shot. Had it been possible to do so, he is certain - as he sits and ponders - that he would have wanted to print and frame the image to set it on his wall, to remind him both where he was and from whence he had come. But just as he was about to fix it in its bath, to settle on it and say "this is me; this represents who I am", Beth had appeared, heralded by her voice, the ultimate echo. And what had she done? On the face of it nothing but enhance his life, his way of living; he assumed he had not needed to compromise anything. But all the while she was seeking to embellish that image by adding sharpness, detail, and - most of all - colour.

The question he had to ask himself - just like that very first question he had posed to Jimmy _____ - was whether or not he wanted colour in his life, because that was what Beth was offering him. Or, even more fundamentally, did he *need* colour in it? Cath had been all about colour; her vision of the photographs they would have hung on their wall was more likely to be landscape than portrait, more vibrant than monotone. And the walls upon which she aspired they should be hung were not those in the lounge of their Kentish Town flat, but above a roaring fireplace in a house in the suburbs. What had Beth said? That she disliked all the places she had lived in London. Neil recalls the conversation they'd had a year earlier when she suggested he should take advantage of his professional success and move out of his Belsize Park flat to somewhere more suitable. And so he had. Slightly further north to a house in Hampstead - fireplaces galore! - funded by his black-and-white life. He remains convinced that she had been motivated only by seeing him advance, more settled, living somewhere more fitting, where he could be happier and contented; after all, she argued, he had managed to garner something akin to status, a status not commensurate with a top-floor conversion just off Haverstock Hill. Any notion that she encouraged him in that direction out of self-interest he has rejected more times than he is aware, rejects it as he does now. Yet there is an open question to be answered. What does Beth want or need, and what part does he play in that?

The voice that tells him she is Cath all over again is a harsh, rasping, wheedling voice; it plays on his old life, his old pain; it drags up images of things he has already rejected - a house, a family; it points to his home in Hampstead and cackles knowingly. Resolutely, he defends Beth against this malignant interloper; not once has she spoken of a shared house, a shared life, marriage, a family. Not once. He believes it an irrefutable defence - and simultaneously believes that not to be the case.

Watching the planes coast into the city, the people on the hill, knowing what he knows about - well - everything, he is certain that the life he is leading, right here and now, is a better life than the one he had been struggling through three or four years earlier. Is it shameful to admit that it is a more contented existence than he had ever enjoyed with Cath? There is a proportion of this newer life he owes to Beth. She has demonstrably changed it - changed *him* - for the better. She has infused his simple philosophy, that developing image, with at least a tint of sepia. There is only one next step: full colour. The voice hisses at him, nagging, its tone weighted, biased; "but what do *you* want, Neil?" it asks, intimating it knows the answer, angling for the banishment of anything that is not monochrome. "When were you truly happy?" it asks. "When were you truly in control?" But Neil knows it isn't all about control. He thinks of the Frisbee, the running dogs, the rounders ball evading the grasp of a fielder. All out of control, yet all adding to the colour of the scene.

So what does he want? Does he know? He thinks so. He believes he is resolved.

Tugged by something invisible, he glances over his shoulder to see Beth appearing over the crest of the hill.

CPSIA information can be obtained
at www.ICGtesting.com
Printed in the USA
BVHW071707250521
608094BV00003B/235